The Mozart Man

Brian Skinner

The Mozart Man

Brian Skinner

Copyright © Brian A Skinner 2022

ISBN: 978-1-7397732-0-5

Written by Brian A Skinner and published by Writersworld, this book is produced entirely in the UK, is available to order from most book shops in the United Kingdom, and is globally available via UK-based Internet book retailers.

Cover Design: Jag Lall

Photo by cottonbro from Pexels
Image by Gerd Altmann from Pixabay
wavebreakmedia/Shutterstock.com
Image by PublicDomainPictures from Pixabay

Copy editor: Sue Croft

WRITERSWORLD
2 Bear Close, Woodstock,
Oxfordshire
OX20 1JX
United Kingdom

www.writersworld.co.uk

The text pages of this book are produced via an independent certification process that ensures the trees from which the paper is produced comes from well managed sources that exclude the risk of using illegally logged timber while leaving options to use post-consumer recycled paper as well.

Dedication

To my wife for her infinite love and patience

To my son Richard for his ideas, suggestions, and
unerring ability to find errors

To my friend, Mike Cartwright who,
the first to plunge into the waters of publication,
encouraged me to do likewise.

CHAPTER 1

The early June evening was warm but the two young men shivered in the gathering darkness as they walked up Greenway in the village of Mallerton. It wasn't exactly a village, not anymore. It had long since been joined to the sprawling town of Temsley. It had a Temsley postcode and used Temsley telephone numbers, but the people who lived there referred to it as 'the Village', as though to associate themselves with Temsley would be demeaning.

Greenway was a very select street. The houses were detached and far enough away from the road and their neighbours as to be almost invisible. Every house had a double garage although most families had more than two cars. Those who lived in Mallerton did not suffer from any sort of financial problems.

"*Someone* down this road must have money in the house," whined the younger of the two men.

"And everyone's got a bloody burglar alarm," snarled his mate.

The pair made odd companions: Louis Green, aged eighteen years, known as Louie the Pole because he was six foot seven inches tall and thin as a rake, and David Tyler, aged twenty-two, known as Tish the Ace because of his onetime ability to cheat at cards without being caught. Both men were heroin addicts and both were becoming more desperate with each passing minute.

"Give us a fag, Louie." They stopped walking and lit up. Nicotine was not a substitute but it was better than nothing at all.

"Let's try this one," whispered Louie urgently. He looked at the sign fixed on the tree. *Slater's Lot* it read. Tish remained silent but his eyes darted nervously from side to side as he looked up and down the street. "Well, let's have a fucking look at least," urged Louie angrily. Tish made up his mind and pushed open the gate.

It was pure chance that they chose *Slater's Lot,* nothing more, nothing less. They weren't to know that the owner was away or that the burglar alarm had been disabled. More importantly, they weren't to know that there was no money at all in the house – and cash was what they were after – Nick Baker only dealt in cash. Walking on the grass to avoid the noise of crunching gravel they moved up to the house. It was in total darkness and there was no sign of any movement. Moving round to the back they checked for lights and movement there, but it was the same – silent as the grave.

They smashed a window and climbed through. The alarm stayed silent, not that they would have cared as desperation cancelled out the need to worry about anything except finding the cash they were after. When they had that in their pockets, Nick Baker would let them have what they wanted so that once again they could tame the craving that burned inside them. The craving caused pain, sweating, and sickness. Only heroin would give them peace.

But there was no money in Charlie Slater's house. As they searched downstairs, they became more and more agitated, dumping the contents of cupboards and drawers onto the floor, where they lay in broken piles. Even the glass cabinets were emptied, their contents smashed and scattered over carpets.

They went upstairs.

"There's no fucking money here," complained Tish as he opened yet another drawer. "D'you reckon Baker would take this?" He lifted up a handful of jewellery and without waiting for a reply began stuffing it in his pockets. Then he pulled the drawer out completely and tipped the remaining items on the bed. Sweeping his arm over the dressing table he sent everything crashing to the floor. They searched everywhere, but there was no sign of any money. In a fit of rage, they tipped over furniture and smashed everything they could see, not worrying about the noise or being caught.

John Bannerman, burglar and all-round thug, had been the man who had disabled the alarm. It was a trademark of his that he fixed the alarm during the daylight hours so that there would be no problems when he came back in the dark. When he arrived at *Slater's Lot,* his chosen and prepared venue, he was surprised to see the lights on. His first thought was that the lights were operated by a time switch, as he knew the owner, who lived alone, was in faraway Bournemouth. The noise, however, convinced him that the house was occupied.

Moving quickly and quietly down to the front of the house he peered in through a front window. He sucked in his breath angrily at the scene that met his eyes. The place was a wreck, and the two men who had made it that way were standing in the centre of it. Bannerman recognised them both and, furious, decided there and then that they would rue the day they had crossed his path. He slipped away unseen, disappearing into the darkness.

The next morning Mrs Ellis, Charlie Slater's housekeeper, arrived as usual for her two-hour stint.

Charlie Slater was enjoying breakfast in the four-star hotel he was staying at and looking forward to closing the deal on his new showroom. Another outlet, especially here in Bournemouth, would mean he could leave Temsley on the pretext of business to relax and breathe in the sea air. He didn't really need an excuse but it would make him feel better. As he poured himself another cup of tea, the waiter came over and told him that he was wanted on the telephone. He stood up, rather surprised, and wondered briefly if the sellers had backed out or received a better offer. It happened.

"Charles Slater." His voice was firm with a trace of public-school accent although he had never attended one, and carried with it an air of authority.

"Mr Slater, it's Mrs Ellis." Her voice wavered and it was obvious to Charlie that she was very upset. "I'm really sorry to tell you this, but you have been burgled."

Charlie was struck dumb at the news. Everything in the house held memories for him – memories of his wife Sue and daughter Karen. Both had been killed on a zebra crossing three years earlier and the thought of someone going through those memories, *stealing* them, made him feel sick.

"Are you still there, Mr Slater?" asked the tremulous voice. He collected himself and with an effort answered her kindly.

"Yes, I'm still here, Mrs Ellis. Have you called the police?"

"Yes, they're at the house now. I'm phoning from next door because they pulled the phones out. The alarm never went off, Mr Slater, but I did set it."

"I'm sure you did, Mrs Ellis. Look, stop worrying and tell the police I'll be home as soon as I can. Meanwhile, you get yourself off home and I'll call you later." He sounded calm, but anger was beginning to burn fiercely and, despite the coolness of the hotel, he was sweating profusely.

The morning's business meeting passed off without a hitch and the deal was settled. Inevitably his thoughts inevitably kept wandering, but if anyone noticed they said nothing. After lunch he checked out of the hotel and set off for home. The June afternoon was hot, but the interior of his Mercedes felt mercifully cool, thanks to the wonders of air conditioning.

The journey took longer than usual, mainly because he found himself reluctant to arrive home. Once there he would have to confront the fact that someone had been in his house and, more importantly, stolen possessions from the past that were dear to his heart, possessions that were irreplaceable. As he neared Temsley he pulled over and called Mrs Ellis at her home. "I'll be home about half past five," he told her. "If you could let the police know, I'd appreciate it." She agreed to inform them and said she would be there too.

At five thirty that evening he turned off the A1 and drove along the Temsley Road. The road followed the line of the river for quite a way but he never gave it a glance. Passing the fire station, he turned left into Mallerton Road. He would be home in just a few minutes now. The car purred softly past the hospital and the college, across the ring road, past Mallerton Hall, then turned left into Greenway. A few seconds later the gates of his house came into view. Flicking the indicator switch almost angrily he turned right into his tree-lined garden.

There was no noise, except the crunching of gravel, as the car moved slowly down the curved drive. He noted, with a sense of remembered satisfaction, the trees that lined the garden where it fronted the road, and recalled vividly Sue's excitement when they were first planted. He smiled at the memory. 'They're there to make sure we have privacy,' she had told him with a smile on her face and a twinkle in her eye. 'We certainly had that,' he thought bitterly, 'and so did those bastards who broke into the house.'

He came to a stop alongside a police car that looked as though it hadn't been washed for months, and switched off the engine. With a growing feeling of dread he climbed out and walked towards the house. Even after five hours' travelling he still looked immaculate. His six-foot frame was upright, military in its bearing. His trousers, with their razor-sharp crease, gave the appearance of having just been pressed. His shoes gleamed, and his white shirt would have a made a good advert for soap powder. His hair was cut short with few signs of greying, and at fifty years old his face was still line free.

Mrs Ellis opened the door to him. She was holding her hands to her face and Charlie could see she had been crying. This was evident when she started to speak.

"Mr Slater," she said softly, her voice wavering nervously over every word, "I'm so very sorry. It was like this when I arrived this morning." A figure appeared behind her, a slender grey-haired man whom Charlie took to be a police officer.

"It's all right, Mrs Ellis," he assured her, "stop worrying."

She looked as though she were about to say something else but the newcomer interrupted her. "Mr Slater?" Charlie nodded. The man held out a warrant card for his inspection. "Inspector Burgess, Temsley CID." Charlie nodded again and went to move past the officer. "I'm afraid it's a bit of a mess, sir."

Charlie stopped and looked into the policeman's face. "A *bit* of a mess?" he queried.

The policeman held his gaze. "It's a hell of a mess."

Charlie stepped into the hallway and stood there unable to believe his eyes. "Oh bloody hell," he muttered. He stood transfixed as his eyes took in the scene.

The house was a large, square, Georgian-style building with six bedrooms. The front door, situated in the centre, opened onto a large hallway. In the middle was a broad staircase with solid oak banister rails that swept upwards in a gracious curve to the rooms above. Two doors on the left of the hall opened into a small but well-stocked library and an office, and on the right to a large dining room and lounge. A door at the back of the staircase led directly into the kitchen and the spacious rear gardens.

Each room had been furnished with the care that only a woman's touch could provide. The hall had boasted an antique walnut table on which stood a large crystal vase containing flowers, and a telephone. A grandfather clock that ticked and chimed away the hours had stood majestically next to it, with oil paintings by a local artist dotted around the walls. The deep pile carpet was ivory in colour, its thickness reminiscent of the best cinemas in the nineteen fifties. Now, everything was wrecked. The walnut table was on its side, a leg broken, the surface covered in deep scratches. The vase lay smashed to smithereens in a sea of trampled flowers. The phone had been ripped out and was lying in pieces against the wall. The grandfather clock lay on its face, shattered, fragments of glass protruding from underneath, its safe comforting ticking now silent. The paintings had been wrenched from the walls and lay in broken heaps on the deep pile carpet. Charlie felt sick.

He looked into his office. His computer was smashed and his files lay scattered and trampled on the floor. In the library, books had been swept from the shelves and lay bent and torn where they had been tossed. The thick pile carpet in dining room was covered in broken glass – the remnants of the lead crystal glassware that had once stood in neat rows in the glass-fronted display cabinet. The dining table, made of yew, highly polished and big enough to seat ten people, stood silently, its surface disfigured by curving scratches like huge grinning lips. The accompanying chairs had been thrown wildly around the room.

He hesitated at the door of the lounge. This was a special room, a room where he could lose himself in the past and be reunited with Sue and Karen. This was the room that Sue had specially chosen to be the 'family' room. Here was where they did their planning and their talking. Here was where Charlie still talked to them both. Surely this room had not been violated? He reached out for the gold-coloured handle. Gentle pressure on his arm made him look round. Mrs Ellis stood there with tears in her eyes, shaking her head slowly, pleading with him not to go in.

"It's just the same in there, Mr Slater," she whispered.

Charlie nodded, pursed his lips and opened the door. He staggered at the sight that met his eyes.

"Why would anyone do this?" he cried. "What's the point?"

Mrs Ellis stayed silent. She knew what the room meant to him and there were no words of comfort that would help him. He walked to the centre of the room ignoring the broken glass and china that lay scattered on the floor. The picture above the fireplace hung lopsided, the glass covered in fractures like spiders' webs, making hideous the three smiling faces that gazed out: Sue, his wife, Karen, his daughter, and himself. This was the last photograph, taken the day before Sue and Karen were killed by a teenager, high on drugs, in a stolen car.

He lifted the picture down gently, as though trying not to hurt the happy people it portrayed, held it close to his chest and wept. Mrs Ellis watched helplessly not knowing what to do. She reached out to him but he just walked round and round the room clutching the picture against him. Sadly she turned away, and as she left the house she asked the police officer to call the doctor out to see the devastated man. She then went home, knowing he would call her when he was ready.

Inspector Burgess came into the room and saw him with the picture. Charlie looked round. "Why?" he cried, "Why? What the hell have I done to deserve this?" The Inspector raised his eyebrows and shook his head slowly, saying nothing. There was nothing he could say that would make any difference. "Come on, Inspector," said Charlie roughly, "you're the expert! What sort of burglar would do this?" He gestured at the damage with his free hand.

"Probably someone who was high on drugs, or desperate for a fix and couldn't find the cash they needed. We should know more when the scenes of crime people have finished."

"You think a drug addict did this?" Charlie's eyes narrowed.

"It's a possibility, that's all."

Charlie Slater suddenly laughed but there was no humour in it.

"That's rich that is, do you know that? First some drug-crazed criminal bastard kills my wife and daughter in a stolen car and now another scumbag addict has smashed up my home and all my memories." He looked at the picture. "What the hell is the world coming to?" He went back into the hallway. "I'm going upstairs," he announced.

"It's just the same up there, sir, I'm afraid."

"I'm still going up there." As Charlie climbed the stairs the Inspector's radio crackled into life informing him that the scenes of crime unit was on its way to him.

CHAPTER 2

He walked slowly up the stairs still clutching the picture tightly to his chest. Looking into each of the rooms he could see the Inspector was right. It was a carbon copy of downstairs, at least as far as the damage was concerned. He went into 'their' room. He hadn't slept there since Sue had died and had kept it just the way it was when she had been alive. Mrs Ellis kept it clean and changed the bedclothes every week just as she had always done. Carefully he removed the photograph and dropped the frame on the floor with the other debris from broken ornaments, scent bottles, and porcelain powder pots. Sitting on the bed he gazed at the picture and whispered, "Someone will pay for this. I promise you both that someone will pay for this… this sacrilege." He pulled a handkerchief from his pocket and dried his eyes, then, with grim determination, he walked downstairs and out to his car.

Standing by the car he ran his fingers along the smooth bodywork. It seemed that this was the only thing in the world belonging to him that hadn't been either damaged or destroyed. The sound of an engine made him look up. A small red van was coming down the driveway towards him. Inspector Burgess hurried outside and seeing the van, commented, "It's the scenes of crime people." Charlie opened his car door. "Do you think you could make a list of everything that's missing, sir?" he added.

Charlie looked at him strangely. "Missing!" he exclaimed loudly. The scenes of crime men, who had started to unload the tools of their trade, stopped what they were doing and looked across at the two men. His voice rose to a shout. "Missing? Everything I own is in there – fucking ruined! I don't give a toss about what's missing."

With a start he realised he had been shouting at this man who, after all, was only trying to do his job and he relented immediately. In a quieter tone he added, "I'm sorry, Inspector, Mrs Ellis will be able to tell you if anything is missing. At the moment all I want to do is get away from here." The policeman nodded understandingly. "I'll let you know where I'm staying when I know myself, but I'll be at the showroom in the High Street during the day." He climbed into the car and started the engine.

The Inspector took two steps back as the car reversed, then watched as it moved silently down the drive with only the crunching of the gravel for accompany it. "I feel sorry for you, Charlie Slater", he muttered, his face grim. "I really do."

He remembered how Mrs Ellis, the sprightly lady who had been the Slater's housekeeper since they had first moved in, had told him of his ways and how he cherished his memories. "This will kill him," she had said. "I don't think he will ever get over this. All his memories are gone and they were all he had left." She had wept all the time she was speaking.

When the car was out of sight the Inspector turned back to the house. He didn't know whether they would arrest anyone for this crime but the wheels were turning now and he would do his best. There was just the chance of an arrest if they could find a decent set of fingerprints. He just hoped Charlie Slater didn't find out who was responsible first.

Pausing in the hallway he dialled a number on his mobile phone. The ringing was answered almost immediately.

"Traffic Wardens office, Jack Templeton."

"Jack, it's Colin Burgess. You're friendly with Charlie Slater, aren't you?"

"I am, yes. Why, what's the problem? I thought he was in Bournemouth."

"He was, but now he's back. His house has been broken into and it's a total wreck. He's just left here and he's taking it very badly. I thought you ought to know."

"Thanks, Colin, I appreciate the call." The Inspector tucked the phone in his inside pocket and went to have words with the SOCO team who were now busy fingerprinting.

Jack Templeton replaced the receiver and gazed thoughtfully into space. He and Charlie had been friends for a long time, over thirty years in fact. It had started in the army. They had joined the same regiment on the same day, and throughout their twenty-two years' service had seen action together in various countries including the Falklands and, of course, Northern Ireland. By the time they retired, Charlie had reached the rank of Major, and Jack, Captain. They knew each other's moods and exactly what each needed in times of stress, and there was no doubt that for Charlie, this would be one of those times.

Picking up the phone again he dialled Charlie's mobile number. It was switched off, but he knew that eventually Charlie would contact him. All he could do for now was wait for that call. Standing by the open window he took out his cigarettes and lit one. He smoked forty a day and was only too aware that in the interests of a long and healthy life, he should give it up. He had made up his mind to do that one day… but not today.

Jack was very much the same build as Charlie and although at fifty-two he was just two years older, he looked nearer sixty. The bags under his eyes were heavier and his hair had decidedly more grey in it, but despite that he was still a reasonably fit man and well able to look after himself. He was the quieter one of the two and never voiced his opinions outside his small circle of friends. Nevertheless he held very decided opinions. His smoking habit, picked up in the army, was something Charlie had never espoused, but Charlie's liking for malt whisky was something Jack too entertained.

Looking across to the river he thought about what Colin had said, that the house was a total wreck. He knew that Charlie had kept everything the way it was when Sue and Karen had been alive and he could easily imagine what he was going through if it was indeed, all wrecked. Glancing at his watch he decided it was time to go home. He would call in at the local shop that lay on his route to get a few extras along with the milk, bread, and bacon – and another bottle of scotch.

Walking along the river to Southbridge Road, as he did every evening and morning, he marvelled at the peaceful riverside scene. It was still very hot, although a gentle breeze ruffled the water and the shadows of the trees provided a welcome coolness that took the edge off the heat. Crossing the bridge, he turned left into the Edgetown estate. This was a small development south of the river, whose boundary went right up to the river's edge. Vandalism had not yet arrived to menace this area of town, although the phone box near the small convenience store was sometimes out of commission. On one occasion the glass had been smashed and it had lain scattered over the footpath like a fall of four-sided hailstones. Thankfully, incidents like that were rare.

As he turned into the square that faced the shop, he was confronted by a group of youths whom he did not recognise. Three boys stood in front of the shop door shouting and trying to impress the three girls who sat on the railings watching them. Unable to get into the shop, Jack stopped and said quietly, "Excuse me." They didn't move. He stared at them, eyes unblinking, his face devoid of expression. Two of them moved away without a word. The third stayed where he was.

"Did you say something?" he sneered. "I didn't 'ear you."

Jack managed to control the urge to grab the youth by his shirt and dump him in the litter bin, and instead leaned forward and whispered, "You won't impress the girls with a bloody nose, lad." The boy paused for a second, shrugged, then shuffled to one side.

When Jack came out of the shop having made his purchases, the group was still hanging around and he heard one of the girls say loudly, "Fuck off, Malcolm, your dick's too small to shag a cat." The other lads sniggered and the girls giggled. He winced inwardly.

"No respect for anyone," he reflected. "Wouldn't have got away saying things like that when I was that age." He made a mental note to call the police when he got home. It was better to stamp on this sort of behaviour right from the start.

When Charlie left the wreck of his house, he drove aimlessly around. He wanted desperately to escape to somewhere but he didn't want to go anywhere in particular. He reasoned that if you didn't have a destination in mind you couldn't arrive, and Charlie didn't want to arrive anywhere just yet. Turning into Mile End Road he drove along the ring road and then off into the poorer part of Temsley. He passed the Carley, Northfield, and Eastley estates then drove over the river via the Southbridge Road.

The June evening was still warm but he wasn't aware of the heat. In fact, he felt cold right through, and shivered as though sickening for the flu. He could not get the picture of his wrecked home out of his mind. He wondered how anyone could do a thing like that. There wasn't any point to it. Was it drug addicts like the Inspector suggested? If it was, something drastic ought to be done. Society should not have to put up with scum like that. He had seen worse damage of course in some of the war-torn countries he had been to, but they were battle zones. Mallerton wasn't a battle zone, it was a quiet residential area where the worst thing that ever happened was someone drinking a little more than they could handle in the pub on a Saturday night, and even that event was a rarity.

He saw a sign indicating a picnic area and turned in that direction. The lane took him down towards the river. The area was deserted. Parking in a bay that faced the water he stared out of the window. He watched as ducks argued and fought at the water's edge, no doubt some territorial dispute. He envied them. He had no territory now and nor did he think he ever would have again. He pulled at his tie, loosened the top button of his shirt, leaned forward on the steering wheel and sobbed, deep wracking sobs that shook his whole body, uncontrollable sobs that started up again and again just as he thought he had cried himself out. Finally he fell into an exhausted sleep.

He awoke with a start. His neck hurt and he was thirsty. It was dark now and a glance at the dashboard clock revealed that it was half past ten. He fumbled in the glove compartment and found his mobile, switched it on and dialled a number. It rang several times and he was about to ring off when there was a click and a voice said, "Jack Templeton."

"Jack," he whispered.

"Charlie – where are you?"

"The house, Jack. It's wrecked."

"I know, Charlie, Inspector Burgess phoned me." There was a brief pause. "Are you all right? Where are you?"

Charlie looked about him, uncertain where he was for a moment. "I'm at some picnic grounds by the river."

"Come over, Charlie, stay with me."

"Oh …Ok, Jack … I'll see you soon." There was another pause and he added, "Thanks." He switched the phone off and dropped it back in the glove compartment before starting the engine and driving towards his friend's house and company.

Charlie caught sight of himself in the long mirror on the wall in the hallway of Jack's house. What a fright he looked.

"I need a wash," he commented.

Jack had already noticed that and replied, "You know where the bathroom is. I'll make the tea."

Ten minutes later Charlie walked into the small lounge looking and feeling a lot better. When he had settled himself in an armchair with a cup of strong sweet tea, he noticed a bottle of Glenmorangie single malt and two glasses on the coffee table. He placed his teacup on the floor. Without a word Jack poured two generous measures of the golden liquid into the glasses and handed one to him. Charlie downed his in one gulp. It was immediately refilled.

Jack said nothing, simply waited for his friend to speak, and when he did he listened without interruption as the damage was described. Although Jack knew that Charlie kept things pretty much as they were when Sue was alive, he didn't know quite the extent to which the house had been a shrine to his wife and daughter. Only his housekeeper knew that. Jack realised that the items in the house could never be replaced, at least not in Charlie's mind. Similar glasses could be found, furniture, carpets, and ornaments replaced with identical ones, but they would not be the ones that he and Sue had bought together. They would not be the ones that Sue had delighted in. Jack realised this, just as he knew that, besides his business, Charlie's whole life had been his wife and little girl. He leaned across the table and refilled the glasses once more.

"It was like a bloody war zone, Jack." Charlie couldn't let it go. "What kind of moron would do something like that?" Jack just shrugged his shoulders and raised his eyebrows. He didn't know the answer to that.

"What was missing?" he asked.

"Missing? That policeman, what's his name …?"

"Colin Burgess."

"Yes, Burgess. He asked me that and could I make a list." Jack nodded. "Truth is, I don't know if anything is missing, it was all so smashed up. He's going to contact Mrs Ellis."

He raised his glass and downed the contents again. The whisky was beginning to have a calming effect.

"Do you want to hear something funny, Jack? He thinks drug addicts were responsible." Jack closed his eyes briefly and thought *Oh shit*. Charlie continued, "I made a vow, Jack." He stretched out the hand holding the glass and Jack immediately splashed more whisky into it. A finger uncurled from round the glass in a pointing gesture and his eyes narrowed. "I made a vow to them both that someone would pay for what happened, and believe me, someone is going to."

Jack believed him but he still asked, "Who? Who will pay?"

"Who?" Charlie looked puzzled. "I don't know who and I don't give a toss either, as long as it's one of those criminal scumbag types, preferably an addict or a pusher." His voice was becoming slurred.

"That's not a good idea, Charlie."

Charlie's head swayed. The whisky on an empty stomach was doing its work.

"Smashing my fucking house up wasn't a good idea either," he retorted. Jack couldn't argue with that.

"Let the police deal with it, Charlie. It's what they're paid for."

Charlie waved the glass in front of him and Jack splashed yet more whisky into it.

"Tell me, what are the chances of the police finding out who did it, eh? What are the chances?"

"About one in three," came the reply, "but that doesn't mean they *won't* find out who's responsible." He could see the effect of the whisky on his friend, which wasn't surprising seeing as the bottle was nearly empty and Jack had only had three tots. "Come on, Charlie, you need some sleep."

"I need revenge." His eyelids were closing.

"You need sleep first. We'll talk about it tomorrow if you want to." He retrieved the glass and put it on the table, then pulled Charlie upright and helped him up the stairs. He flopped onto the bed and, as Jack pulled his shoes off, he muttered, "Tomorrow, Jack. Promise?"

Jack pulled the duvet over him. "I promise," he whispered, but Charlie never heard him, he was out like a light.

CHAPTER 3

The following morning Charlie woke up to the smell of frying bacon and for a moment he thought he was back in the army. Sitting on the edge of the bed he squinted at his watch. It was six fifteen. His mouth was dry and his head hurt like hell. With an effort he stood up and stripped off his clothes, then padded out to the bathroom and stood under a cold shower.

When the cold water had washed away the fuzziness in his head, if not the pain, he switched the control to hot and cleansed himself of the previous day's dirt, then towelled himself dry and padded back into the bedroom where he shaved. He felt much better even though the quiet hum of the razor sounded like a roar. Having dressed, he made his way down the narrow staircase, following his nose to where the bacon was sizzling. Headache or no, nothing would put him off a plate of crispy bacon.

Jack had heard him coming and had already poured out a cup of hot strong tea to which he added two heaped spoonfuls of sugar. "Cup of tea on the table," he said as Charlie walked into the small kitchen, "and bacon coming up."

Charlie sat down and began to sip at the hot tea, both hands wrapped round the cup. A plate of bacon was put in front of him.

"Help yourself to bread and butter," and putting a bottle of paracetamol tablets on the table, Jack added, "and take two of those."

A wry smile tugged at Charlie's mouth. "You think of everything, don't you?"

"Army training," quipped Jack.

The two men ate in silence. Charlie couldn't remember the last time he had eaten a plate of crispy bacon with fresh bread and butter except when he had been in the army. When they had finished eating Jack poured out two more cups of tea, lit up his third cigarette of the day and asked. "What are you going to do? About the house, I mean."

"Do?" The look of anger that flitted across Charlie's handsome features was quickly replaced by a look of sadness. "I'll do nothing. What can I do? I can't go back. There's nothing there for me now." He paused. "I'll get the insurance people down and then I'll put it on the market." He started to collect the cups and plates and pile them into the sink.

"Leave that, Charlie. I'll do it later."

"No, let me. Anyway, later I want to talk about revenge."

Jack had known that was coming. No matter how drunk Charlie got, and he had seen him drunk more than a few times, he never forgot what he had been talking about before he finally flaked out.

As Charlie washed up, Jack made yet another pot of tea and they both settled at the small table and looked searchingly at one another. Each waited for the other to speak. Jack lit up another cigarette and inhaled deeply.

"Those things are not a good idea," Charlie commented with a frown, indicating the cigarettes.

Jack nodded. "Maybe," he acknowledged, blowing smoke, "but revenge isn't a good idea either. It might be different if you knew who did it, but in that case you would risk being recognised. Then what?"

"All right, maybe revenge isn't a good idea, but things are getting out of hand around here. What do you think about handing out some justice? Real justice I mean, not what the bloody do-gooders call justice."

Jack sipped his tea. "Who will you hand this 'justice' out, eh? How many criminals do you know?"

"You work in a police station, Jack. You could get information on the local scumbags."

Jack considered that for a moment. Getting the information would be easy enough. He had access to the computer system, albeit limited access, but he was certain he would be able to get the passwords needed to log on to the files. The passwords policemen thought up, especially CID, were laughable – their own telephone numbers, the names of their children, wives and dogs. There were even the names of a couple of mistresses being used. Yes, getting the information should not pose much of a problem. "But even if you had the information it wouldn't do you much good. You can't dish out justice in the street and you would have a great problem picking anyone up. Do you really think anyone would come with you voluntarily!"

Charlie looked over the rim of his cup and smiled smugly. "If we were in police uniform there would be no problem."

"What about being recognised? Uniform or not, practically everyone in town would recognise you from a hundred yards." Charlie drained his cup and put it slowly down on the table. "There's always Lucy."

Jack just nodded, a look of resignation spreading across his face. He knew Charlie would be resolute in his pursuit of payback, but he didn't realise how determined until he mentioned Lucy. She was his younger sister and, as far as Jack knew, his only living relative. Jack had a soft spot for Lucy and had since he first met her. She was the one woman he trusted completely.

Lucy Slater who, at five foot nine was considered fairly tall, wasn't without appeal, but she was flat chested and plain-featured. She would never make a page three girl. Her short hair was as black and shiny as a raven's wing and her small, line-free face made her look younger than her thirty-six years, although the heavy glasses she wore did nothing to set off her looks. She was very slim and would have had a nice figure except for lack of a bust. She was also a first-class makeup artist with a reputation in theatre and television that was second to none.

Jack had first met her when home on leave with Charlie. She was fourteen then and still a gangly schoolgirl. He was thirty. They got on well, but of course she was only a child. At Charlie's wedding, eight years later, she had changed and they had what was known as a 'bit of a fling'. Unfortunately, Jack felt guilty about the sexual feelings she aroused in him, not just because she was sixteen years younger but because she was Charlie's sister. As a result, although their friendship was firmly established, romance never quite showed itself above the horizon.

There had been other occasions when they met up – when Karen was born, the christening, various birthdays, and of course when Sue and Karen were killed. Lucy had dropped everything and hurried down to be with her brother in his time of need. She and Sue had been very good friends right from the moment they met, and Aunt Lucy had been a great favourite of Karen's. Their loss had been almost as big a blow to her as to Charlie. There was no doubt in Jack's mind that Lucy would do everything in her power to help her brother get revenge, or dish out justice, as he called it.

Jack stubbed out his cigarette and poured another cup of tea. He indicated the pot to Charlie, who shook his head.

"Does she know about the house yet?"

Sadness was still etched on Charlie's face as he replied, "Not yet. I'll call her later today. I'm sure she'll help us, Jack."

'Us! He's using the word 'us' already,' thought Jack in some trepidation. He leant back in his chair. "Of course she would help, but is it really fair to involve her?"

If Charlie could have looked any more wretched it would have been at that moment. He considered the question for a minute. "Fair? Probably not. But if I didn't involve her, or at least give her the chance to be involved, that wouldn't be fair either. If I tried to do something single-handed I know she would feel let down."

He picked up the empty tea cup and looked inside as though the answer to all his problems would somehow be written there. He looked up at his friend. "Come on, Jack, you know Lucy, you know what she's like."

Jack nodded. He knew what she was like all right. He changed the subject. "Look, I have to be at work soon." He rummaged in a little wooden bowl that stood on the fridge. Pulling a key from it he placed it on the table. "Come and go as you like. I'll pick up a Chinese on the way home. Eight o'clock suit you?"

"Fine," came the reply. "I'll see you later." Jack picked up his coat and went to the door. "You know where I am if you want me," he called. Charlie nodded.

Jack closed the door and was gone, whistling a tune. He had a small car but he never used it to go to work, except in adverse weather conditions, and today was definitely walking weather. It was already very warm and all set to be another hot day.

Crossing the bridge he followed the far bank of the river. The water was flat calm like a mirror, the only movement being the ripples left by swans as they swam gracefully up stream. At this time of the morning, on a summer's day such as this, it was hard to imagine that there was an undercurrent of malicious criminal activity bubbling away in Temsley, or that during the previous night there had probably been several burglaries and untold criminal damage, and no doubt during the coming day there would be arrests for shoplifting and car theft. He crossed the grass and headed for the rear entrance of the police station.

One of the first things he did was to seek out Colin Burgess. He wanted to see for himself the devastation his friend had described and find out whether there were any clues to the identity of those responsible. The Inspector showed no surprise when Jack asked if he could see the house, knowing as he did what firm friends they were.

"I'm going there shortly," he said, "to see Mrs Ellis. She said she's made a list of things that are missing. She also wants to start clearing up, I think. See me in the yard in twenty minutes." Jack thanked him and went to get a cup of tea.

He was sitting at his desk sipping the brown liquid that passed for tea from the machine in the canteen, when one of the typists came in and gave him a letter. "Thought this might be urgent," she told him. He looked up, smiled his thanks, and watched the gentle sway of her buttocks as she turned and left. *You're getting to be a dirty old man, Templeton*, he told himself as he tore open the brown envelope. It was notification of a court case that involved one of his wardens, Ronnie Thompson, who had been assaulted. It was more than urgent as the hearing was for the next day and Ronnie was on two days' leave. He finished the tea, pulled a face, and dropped the polystyrene cup into the waste bin before making his way to the back yard and Colin Burgess.

"How is Charlie Slater now?" Burgess asked as they turned into Mallerton Road and headed for the more upmarket part of the town. "He looked bloody awful yesterday."

"He got drunk at my place last night and he's got a sod of a headache this morning although he won't admit it." Changing the subject he asked, "Any ideas as to who might have done it?"

"Ideas! Got them by the bucketful, but no evidence as yet." Jack pulled out his cigarettes and offered him one which he took. After he lit up he added, "I don't ever remember seeing damage as bad as that before. I'd say they were amateurs - probably drug addicts – but there's a problem with that."

"Problem?"

"Yes. The alarm didn't go off and when we checked we discovered it had been doctored. Looked like a professional job too, and professionals don't make that sort of mess."

"Surely if a pro had fixed the alarm he would have been in."

"Depends. There's one chap in particular that fixes the alarm in daylight and comes back when it's dark."

"Bannerman!" declared Jack.

Colin Burgess was impressed but shook his head. "He wouldn't do anything like what was done to Charlie Slater's house. Anyway, how does a traffic warden know about Bannerman?"

"Come on, Colin. I've worked in the nick for over ten years. I know about most of the scumbags. We get the intelligence bulletins as well, you know."

The car turned left into Greenway and the entrance to the drive came into view. The indicator ticked monotonously as they waited for an approaching car to pass them.

"Come on, for God's sake," muttered the policeman. The car drove by and they turned into the drive.

As they approached the door it opened and Mrs Ellis stood there, an envelope in her hand. She looked at Jack and smiled weakly. "Hello, Mr Templeton. Have you seen Mr Slater?"

Jack smiled back. "Yes, he's staying with me for a while, Mrs Ellis. He's fine, so don't worry."

She turned to the policeman and handed him the envelope. "Here's that list you wanted," she told him. "As far as I can see, it's only jewellery that's gone. Everything else is … smashed."

Colin took the envelope, tucked it in his pocket and said quietly, "We've finished in the house, Mrs Ellis, so if you want to clear up, you can."

Jack drew in a deep breath as they walked into the hallway. "Christ," he said, "Charlie was right, it *is* like a war zone." He looked about him. "What are all those grey patches?" he asked.

"Aluminium dust. The SOCO use it on fingerprints – and before you ask – we lifted four sets. One was Mrs Ellis's, another will be Mr Slater's although we need to take his prints for elimination purposes, and the other two sets will be our villains. If they're on record we'll soon know, but don't bank on it."

"Are all the rooms like this?"

Colin nodded. "Some are actually worse."

"Bloody hell, no wonder he was in such a state."

They stayed for about ten minutes during which time Jack looked in all the downstairs rooms. He thought he had seen enough in his lifetime not to be shocked at anything people did, but this took his breath away. 'There has to be an answer to this sort of crime,' he thought to himself. 'Maybe Charlie's right, perhaps we should dish out some rough justice and let everyone know why we're doing it. It might stop the rot.' When they went back outside Jack felt relieved, as though he had come to a decision. He lit up another cigarette.

"Can you do me a favour, Colin, and drop me at Westfield Road? I've got to see Ronnie Thompson."

"Isn't he the traffic warden who was assaulted?"

"That's him. The case comes up tomorrow and he doesn't know about it yet."

Westfield Road consisted of two rows of terraced houses on the Northfield Estate and Ronnie Thompson lived with his mother at number 41 On the outside, the houses were neat and clean. Each had a six-foot-long garden at the front bordered by a three-foot-high brick wall. Some of the gardens were given over to colourful flower beds, others boasted a large bushy plant surrounded by stone chippings, and one or two were gravelled over completely. Rowan trees graced the footpath every thirty yards or so. The street lamps were electric but they reminded Jack of the old-fashioned gas lights he knew as a child. The many different types and colours of gates, broke the monotony of the garden walls.

Number 41 was at the corner of The Way, a link road that joined Westfield Road to Northfield Road and allowed access to the rear gardens of both streets. Its front garden was full of flower beds and was a blaze of colour. It was the first time Jack had called at Ronnie's house and he noticed that the paint work was clean, the windows sparkled, and the flowered curtains looked as though they were freshly laundered. Mrs Thompson invited him in. Inside was the same as the outside, neat, clean, and tidy.

Jack passed on the message about the court appearance and while they drank a cup of tea that Jack wasn't given the opportunity to refuse, Ronnie made known his very definite opinions about what he thought certain punishments should be. He was very right-wing in his views and Jack wondered whether it was just talk or whether he would actually do some of the things he talked about. There was really no way of knowing until it came to the crunch and the chances of that happening were almost nil. Still, he learnt a lot about Ronnie Thompson and his points of view. One thing was becoming clear to him – Charlie's notion of dishing out so-called justice in an effort to reduce the crime rate was another step nearer to becoming a reality.

Having thanked Mrs Thompson for the tea and said goodbye, he walked back to the police station. He could not get the devastation at Charlie's house out of his mind and had difficulty concentrating on the meetings that he had to attend. It was therefore a huge relief when at seven-thirty he finally finished for the day and left the police station. Walking home he called in at the Chinese takeaway for a set meal for two, after which he stopped at the local shop for a bottle of red wine, noticing that there was no sign of the youths that had been there the previous day. At his front door he fumbled with his key and dropped it. Cursing under his breath he stooped to retrieve it. When he straightened up the front door was open and Lucy Slater stood framed in the doorway.

"Hello, Jack."

She smiled at him and he remembered with amazing clarity his enjoyment of the last time they had met. Although he had known she would want to come straight over on hearing about her brother, he hadn't known when. His heart pounded just that little bit quicker.

"Lucy," he cried, trying to sound surprised and failing. The surprise would have been had she not been there. "It's good to see you again." She reached over and took the bottle from him, kissing him on the cheek as she did so.

"Here, let me take that." She turned and walked into the house. Jack followed, shutting the door with a neat flick of his foot.

She was the only woman he had ever completely trusted, not

that he knew many really well. She was everything he ever wanted in a woman, but the sixteen-year age gap and the fact that she was Charlie's sister was still somehow a taboo to him. He knew deep down it was illogical, but he kept seeing her as she was when he first met her and she was only fourteen. He had a fear too of being rejected, so was at pains not to get involved, even though he badly wanted to. He wondered if he would still be able to hide his feelings for her, something he had successfully managed in the past … maybe she didn't think of him that way, maybe she … He didn't want to contemplate any other maybes – better to take things as they came along.

"Where's Charlie?" he asked. "This meal is only for two."

"He phoned to say he won't be back tonight," Lucy told him. "Something to do with the new showroom he's opening." She took the foil containers from him and looking straight into his eyes, added, "It's just you and me tonight, Jack." His heart beat faster than ever.

CHAPTER 4

It was another beautiful June day, cloudless and warm with just the merest hint of a breeze. It was the sort of day to be outside, which was a pity, at least for Jack Templeton and Ronnie Thompson. Both had to appear at the magistrates' court to give evidence in the assault case in which Ronnie was the victim and Jack a witness.

Although the courthouse was a fairly recent building, it had soon got very run-down and looked decidedly tatty. The tables and chairs in the waiting area were greasy, and miscreants waiting to be called had carved their names on them, likewise the door panels. Metal litter bins were dotted here and there, and although not full, the floor space surrounding them was covered in plastic cups, cigarette ends, and old magazines. The painted walls were grubby and in desperate need of a wash, and the floor tiles were littered with flattened pieces of chewing gum and pools of spilt tea. It was also oppressively hot, even though the large windows that made up a good deal of the front of the building were tinted to stop the worst of the burning sun from streaming through.

Carefully avoiding the debris, the two men picked their way across the waiting area towards the police room where they would stay until called. Being dressed in the uniform of traffic wardens meant they had to endure the hostile remarks of some of those waiting to be brought before 'their worships' on various charges ranging from non-payment of fines to being drunk and disorderly, and assault. One particularly dirty and scruffy individual with a shaved head, several earrings in his ears and one hanging from his nose, sneered at the pair, showing black and decaying teeth. "What's it like to be a prat, then?" he sniggered.

Ronnie stopped, stared at him, then replied quietly, "You ought to know, you've had more practice than me."

The sneer turned to a scowl and the scruff muttered 'Bollocks' before turning away.

Dave Turner, the man who had assaulted Ronnie, was among those waiting, but he was tucked away in a corner deep in conversation with a smartly dressed man who was his solicitor, and failed to notice their arrival. Ronnie saw him and was surprised at the change in his appearance. Gone was the four-day stubble, the scruffy jeans and tee-shirt that Ronnie remembered, and gone was the long greasy hair and bushy sideburns. Instead, there was a smart, clean-shaven young man with short shiny hair, wearing a white shirt and a tie. His grey suit was neatly pressed and his black shoes highly polished. Despite the difference, however, he was still recognisable. Ronnie nudged Jack.

"I know," he commented. "I spotted him."

When they reached the comparative safety and quiet of the police waiting-room they eased themselves gratefully into the low chairs that always seemed to be the norm in public buildings, and talked about nothing in particular. This was only the second time that Ronnie had been to court to give evidence, the first being about a disputed parking ticket, and he was understandably nervous. He kept glancing at the clock on the wall as if by doing so the time would pass more quickly. After an hour and a half Ronnie decided that it was time to relieve himself of some of the tea he had been drinking, but as he stood up the usher put her head round the door.

"You're on next," she told them.

"Well, sod me! Ronnie exclaimed, "Just when I'm dying for a piss."

Jack smiled. "Sod's law, that," he remarked. They both stood up, combed their hair, brushed imaginary specks of dust off their jackets and walked out to court number 3. Ronnie was called in almost immediately.

Jack checked his pockets to make sure that everything was in order, even though he knew it was. He tapped his breast pocket and felt the oddly comfortable bulk of his notebook. His fingers touched the top of the large paper clip that he had used to mark the correct page. The usher opened the door and he walked towards her, expecting to be called, However, she caught his eye and shook her head. It was then that he saw Ronnie emerge from the varnish and polish of the courtroom, anger and disbelief on his face. He said nothing, just headed for the police waiting room and the toilet. Jack followed.

As he emerged from the toilet he said, "That was quick. What happened?"

Ronnie threw his notebook on the table. It slid across the shiny surface and fell to the floor, its pages rustling angrily. Jack tried again. "Ronnie, what happened?"

Ronnie spun round. "Happened? Nothing happened. The bastard got away with it. A technicality they said, a computer error or something. Who cares? All I know is that the bastard thumped me and got away with it. Fucking magistrates are useless." He bent forward to retrieve the notebook.

"Surely it was adjourned?" argued Jack.

"No, dismissed. No case to answer and the prosecution offered no evidence. That clever bastard defending him highlighted some lack of procedure or an error, and BINGO!"

Jack too felt a surge of anger and disappointment, but he had seen too many cases thrown out of court, and the decisions of magistrates had long ago ceased to surprise him. He sympathised with Ronnie but there was nothing he could do about it.

"Come on, I'll buy you a cup of tea." Ronnie looked up, shook his head angrily and rolled his eyes heavenwards. "He won't get away with it, Jack."

"There's nothing you can do. Come on, let's get that cuppa."

Ronnie stood still. "Nothing? Oh yes there is, Jack. I know who he is and where he lives. He'll have both his legs broken before a week passes and that's a promise."

Jack's voice became stern. "I'm not hearing this, now come on." He pushed open the door and together they crossed the waiting area. It was almost empty now, and apart from a depressed-looking cleaner who dabbed half-heartedly at the tea spills with his mop, there were only one or two people left waiting to see what the magistrates had in store for them.

On the steps outside in the warm sunshine, Dave Turner, the man who had assaulted Ronnie and got off on a 'technicality', was laughing with one of his mates. He saw them as they approached and sneered, daring them to say something. Ronnie tensed and slowed down but Jack pushed him in the back, forcing him forward.

"Keep going or you'll buy the teas." They made their way back to the police station canteen where Jack bought two cups of the machine brew and headed toward a corner table.

Although he managed to give the opposite impression, Jack was in fact in favour of someone breaking Dave Turner's legs. He himself had been brought up very strictly as a child. His parents had laid down guidelines for their children and if they were crossed, they were punished immediately. He had two sisters and one brother, and all of them found out the hard way what the punishment was. Jack was now of the opinion that the law was crazy and far too lenient. The so-called deterrents that politicians spoke of were non-existent, in his view. Even when criminals were found guilty and sent to prison, life wasn't exactly hard. Prisons today he considered were more like hotels – three meals a day plus facilities and opportunities that a lot of law-abiding citizens on the outside would have gladly taken advantage of. Working in a police station had served to harden his opinion on the subject, although he would never have dreamed of voicing his views, or of going outside the law. He was beginning to dream now, though. Maybe Charlie was right.

He thought back to the number of 'scumbag youths' that had come into the police station for their official 'cautions'. He knew, as did the police, that most of them would go back on the streets and behave in exactly the same way. They had no shame, any of them. Even those that were sentenced showed little or no remorse. The punishment, if that's what it could be called, would invariably be community service, or a fine which the tax payer paid as the offenders were usually on benefits of some kind. He could never understand why magistrates, or anyone else, thought that community service, which often consisted of gardening jobs, cutting hedges or sweeping up, usually in homes for the elderly, was a punishment. If he had his way they would be birched, or made to do pointless hard labour such as moving a pile of boulders from one place to another and then back again for fourteen hours a day. As for prison conditions – well!

He was suddenly aware that Ronnie was asking him if he was all right. He smiled. "I'm fine. Just thinking."

"Anything interesting?"

"All my thoughts are interesting." There was no way he

would let Ronnie know his true feelings. It wasn't something you made public if you worked in a police station. He stood up. "Right, let's get back to work." He threw the polystyrene cups into the bin.

"Right," said Ronnie, "I'll see you later." He made his way to the street and his patrol. Jack went to his office and a pile of paperwork. 'Maybe ...,' he thought. 'Yes, I'll try to find out more about Dave Turner or even John Bannerman.'

In the afternoon, because it was a Friday and very busy, Jack toured the streets in the town centre. He liked to make sure that his staff were where they should be and to help out with any unforeseen problems. As he neared the pelican crossing by the post office he heard a thump, then women screaming. He knew without thinking about it that someone had been knocked down. Pushing his way through the crowd that had gathered, he could see a man's body underneath a stationary vehicle, the legs protruding from between the wheels. Stabbing his finger on the transmit button of his radio, he called for police help and an ambulance. He walked round to the driver's side where the head and shoulders were visible. The driver's door was open and the car empty. A woman, obviously the driver, sat on the island in the centre of the road, sobbing. Another woman had her arms round her trying to comfort her.

Seeing Jack in his uniform she stopped crying and called out, "He just jumped out in front of me." She shook her head. "I couldn't stop in time, it wasn't my fault," and she burst out crying once more. Jack knelt down and felt for a pulse in the victim's neck, being careful not to move the head. He found one. With a shock he realised that the man was Dave Turner. He pressed the transmit button again and informed control that the victim was alive, unconscious, and trapped beneath a vehicle.

"Can you see what sort of injuries there are?"

"Negative," he replied, "but it looks like the vehicle has gone over both legs and maybe the chest too."

The wail of the ambulance siren could be heard and Jack looked up to see how bad the traffic was. A police officer arrived on the scene, and as the crowd parted to let him through, he caught a glimpse of someone, wearing a civilian jacket, who looked suspiciously like Ronnie Thompson. He made to go after him but the crowd closed up and the figure was lost to view.

'What the hell was he doing here?' he thought, 'and why wasn't he in uniform?'

"Can you get some of this traffic moving, Jack?" called the newly-arrived police officer. Immediately he started to do just that, making sure the first two or three cars were pulled over to one side so that the officer could question the drivers. The ambulance, siren blaring, sped up the High Street, forcing the traffic to move over. Once it had arrived on the scene, the medics took control of the situation and decided the man had possible neck injuries and could not be moved. The car would have to be lifted.

As Jack got the traffic moving again, he began to puzzle over the appearance of Ronnie Thompson. Was it him he saw? He should have been on a patrol over a mile away. Was it merely coincidence that Dave Turner was the victim and Ronnie just happened to be in the vicinity? He didn't believe in that sort of coincidence and decided to tackle him about it when they met up again next day.

The following morning Ronnie came into the office and shut the door. Jack studied him for a moment. He didn't look worried or concerned as to what this interview was about. Jack looked at some papers on his desk, letting him sweat for a moment. Finally, Ronnie broke the silence. "Why do you want to see me, Jack, have I done something wrong?"

Jack looked up from the papers. "We both know the answer to that, Ronnie."

The traffic warden tried to look baffled. "Come on, Jack, what's this all about?"

Jack leaned forward slightly. "You just had to do it, didn't you? You couldn't leave it."

Alarm registered on Ronnie's face. "What are you talking about?" His voice had dropped to a whisper.

"You were seen, Ronnie. What was it – a push? Or did you stick a pin in him? A quick jab in the leg at the right moment and it would look like he jumped out in front of the car that hit him."

Ronnie just stared for a moment saying nothing, then he too leaned forward, a look of anger suffusing his face.

"Well, he asked for it, the bastard. The only thing I'm sorry about is that he won't know it was me who did it." He paused and the anger drained from him. "Who saw me?"

"*I* did, you prat. I saw you. I don't know if anyone else did but I'm sure the closed-circuit television cameras will have picked you up."

"What are you going to do?"

"I don't know yet. Get back on your patrol and let me think about it."

"Whatever you do, Jack, I know I was right. There are too many do-gooders and they've been at it too long. All they've proved is that their methods don't work. What *I* did works, at least for that bastard Turner."

"How did you know he was going to be there at that time?"

"I heard him telling his mate when they left court."

"Think yourself lucky he's not dead, Ronnie. Close the door on your way out."

Jack had known from the first that he was not going to report him for causing the accident that put Dave Turner in hospital. The only reason he said anything at all was to find out if he could be trusted and whether he was prepared to go further when it came to handing out rough justice. He still wasn't sure about him, but he knew he would find out one way or another. If Ronnie was willing, plans could be made for some real justice to be handed out. The more he thought about it, the more he convinced himself it was a worthwhile scheme and the right thing to do.

He stood by the open window, lit a cigarette and gazed out towards the river. It was difficult to equate the peaceful scene he saw with the criminal activity in Temsley that was getting worse with each passing day.

CHAPTER 5

While Jack and Ronnie were in court, the Sharks were wandering the streets. There were four of them and they called themselves the Sharks because Craig, the eldest, had seen them in the film West Side Story and thought it was a 'cool' name. Craig Thomas was thirteen and his brother Mark eleven. Both were big for their age and sported skinhead haircuts, an earring in the left ear, trainers, jeans and dirty tee-shirts. They had been excluded from school because of what the education authorities called 'behavioural problems'. In addition they had convictions for shoplifting and criminal damage – mostly graffiti, and many local bus shelters and telephone kiosks had felt the touch of their destructive hands. Their parents had never bothered with them and the social services had all but given up.

The remaining two Sharks were girls. One, Amanda Green aged thirteen, was a pretty girl who could easily pass for sixteen. She had collar-length auburn hair that gleamed in the light and a figure that most girls could only dream of. She was intelligent, but bored with the routine of school life. She craved excitement. She also had a crush on Craig and played truant to be with him, thinking that the outrageous things he did were far more exciting than school books. Her parents were kindly, well-meaning people who had no idea what motivated a thirteen-year-old girl, so they bought her whatever she wanted and assumed she was 'going through a phase' when they found out she had missed school or there was money missing from the house.

Wendy Miles was twelve and what's known as a 'tom boy'. She could run faster, play football better, and climb trees higher than any of the boys. She could also fight with a ferocity that even the boys shied away from. At school she was an under-achiever, easily frustrated with things she had difficulty understanding, and as a result was a slow learner. To avoid the frustration, she played truant. She enjoyed being a 'Shark' because she thought it gave her a modicum of status among the other children on the Eastley Estate where all four of them lived, although of late she was becoming bored even with them. She didn't like being a girl. Her developing breasts were a nuisance and her periods, which had just started, were messy and painful, but most of all she was getting attention from her stepfather that she did not want. He had taken to making suggestive remarks to her and was always coming into her room when she was dressing or changing her clothes. She had thought about telling her mother, but, as her only interest seemed to be bingo, she knew she would not be believed. She had vowed that if he ever actually tried to do anything she would stick a knife in him.

"Anyone got a fag?" she asked as they crossed the recreation ground opposite Bradley Street. Mark pulled out a crumpled packet from his pocket.

"What's it worth?" he taunted, waving it in front of her.

"What do you want?"

"You know what I want."

"Yeah, well you can piss off. I have enough with that dirty old sod at home without you starting." Mark handed her a cigarette and threw her a box of matches. As she lit up, he asked,

"Has he done it to you yet?"

"No, he bloody well hasn't," she snapped, "but he's working up to it." She threw the matches back and he too lit up.

"You want to tell someone," Craig told her. "He could be put away." He looked at his brother and beckoned to him. Mark threw him the cigarettes and matches too.

"Who am I going to tell? Mum won't believe me and neither will them bitchy teachers at school." She sucked on the cigarette and inhaled deeply. "I wouldn't tell a man teacher either, he'd probably want to do it to me an' all, dirty lot of sods."

"My Dad hasn't done anything like that," chimed in Amanda, "and I'm older than you."

"Well, he's your dad, isn't he? I mean, he wouldn't do anything like that." She spat on the ground. "This bloke's my stepdad so it's not the same, is it?"

Squeezing through the fence they walked up the service road and through an alley into Eastfield Road, then down to the High Street where they stopped to gaze at the cars on display in Slater's Showroom.

"I like that one," said Craig, pointing to a low-slung bright red Mazda sports car.

"Not enough room in the back," remarked Amanda, "not for what I want to do, anyway." Mark sniggered and Craig shot him a *keep your mouth shut* look. Undaunted Mark laughed.

"He's too scared to do it, Mandy," he taunted and added, "but I'm not."

Amanda looked at Mark with disgust. "You're just a little boy," she cried contemptuously, "and a disgusting one." Craig had walked off in a huff and Amanda now followed him. Wendy and Mark followed at a safe distance, knowing that Craig would lash out at his brother given the chance, and Wendy too if she happened to get in the way.

They turned into the park and followed the footpath. Although it was a warm June day it was surprisingly empty of people. Craig reached up and broke an overhanging branch off a tree. Trailing it behind him he continued to walk towards the railway bridge. As they crossed it, he lifted the branch in the air and without looking heaved it over the edge onto the lines below. Amanda giggled and Mark pulled himself up on the parapet to see where it landed. Wendy showed no reaction, but the sudden realisation came into her mind that Craig was a prat, and with that thought she discovered she was bored. She wondered briefly if she would be bored had she gone to school.

They carried on walking until they reached the footbridge that spanned the dual carriageway ring road, at which point they all started to collect stones. Some were quite large, almost house brick size, but most were only pebbles. Wendy joined in, more out of habit than because she wanted to, and by then she was beginning to have second thoughts about the things they were doing.

They stood at the start of the bridge with their arms full of stones, waiting for Craig to give the word. He looked up the road waiting for a number of vehicles to approach – one car or lorry on its own was no fun. A group of about nine vehicles came speeding towards the bridge and everyone tensed up.

"Now!" called Craig, and he, Amanda, and Mark rushed onto the bridge and hurled their loads into space, watching as they rained down on the traffic below. Only Wendy stayed where she was and she dropped her stones on the ground where she stood.

The first car in the fast lane received a direct hit from one of the larger stones. It bounced off the bonnet and shattered the windscreen. The car careered sideways, crashed into the central reservation as the driver fought for control and then flipped over onto its roof. Two or three of the drivers had seen the children on the bridge and started to brake, but it was no use. They were all driving too fast and too close together to avoid a collision and the result was a nine-car pileup.

The Sharks ran off the way they had come, laughing. They went back into Green Park, through the underpass and then climbed over the fence surrounding the Northway Retail Park. As they did so they could hear the sirens of the emergency services screaming down the road.

"One of them must have had a mobile phone," shouted Amanda. "Yuppie bastard!"

Wendy, however, was concerned that someone could have been hurt or even killed in the mayhem they had just caused, and bravely voiced her fears. "What if someone was killed back there?"

Craig glared at her. He had noticed that she hadn't taken part in the stone dropping.

"Don't tell me you're going soft!" He scratched his head. "It was their own fault anyway. They were all driving too close."

"And too fast," chimed in Amanda.

Wendy wasn't happy. "I just don't think we should have done it, that's all. Not with that many cars."

The pileup had blocked the south-bound carriageway completely and by the time the emergency services arrived there was a queue of traffic a mile long. It was an hour before all the injured had been taken to hospital. Two of them had to be cut out of their cars and were in a serious condition. Nine more were kept in overnight, and the rest were sent home after treatment to cuts and bruises. The police had managed to get statements from those only slightly injured and also from two drivers who saw the episode but were travelling in the opposite direction. Although they all said that the stone throwers were children and that there were three of them, they were unable to give any detailed descriptions as they were either too far away, or too busy trying to avoid a collision.

Dave Saunders, a uniformed sergeant, surveyed the damage and shook his head sadly. He was surprised that no one had been killed. At least three of the vehicles were complete write-offs and the others were all badly damaged. He was almost certain he knew who was responsible, but proving it would be practically impossible.

The constable who had driven Dave to the scene wondered, "Who do you reckon would do a thing like this, Skip?"

His sergeant replied grimly, "Without a doubt – Craig Thomas and his brother Mark. This is just the sort of thing they do, amongst others. There's normally a couple of girls tagging along with them – Amanda Green and Wendy Miles. They call themselves the Sharks and they're a right bunch of toe rags, no mistake."

The Sharks, meanwhile, had sauntered into the shopping centre where they were successful in stealing cans of spray paint. From there they crossed Northway and dawdled into the Gallfield Estate where they decorated telephone kiosks, bus stops and some junction boxes belonging to the cable television companies, before making their way back to the Eastley Estate and their home ground.

It was hot and Craig had begun to wish they had stolen cans of drink instead of spray paint. Knowing that his house would be empty he made a decision. "Come on, we'll go back to my place."

"Our place," corrected Mark.

"Oh goodie," chimed in Amanda looking directly at Craig.

Wendy turned to Mark. "We might be going to your house but keep your hands to yourself," she warned.

"You don't mean that," he sneered, eyeing her up and down.

"Just don't try anything, that's all."

Mark tried to look unconcerned, but he couldn't understand why Wendy kept saying no, especially when her friend Amanda was so keen to do it with Craig. Then again, he couldn't understand why Craig didn't bonk Amanda at every opportunity.

The Thomas's house was a tip. The carpet needed vacuuming and the paintwork needed washing, along with the net curtains, which were grey instead of white and torn in places. The windows were covered with the dirt and dust of many months and the three-piece suite, which was badly stained, needed a thorough steam clean. All the ashtrays were full, and the whole house stank of stale tobacco smoke. Newspapers and magazines lay around in jumbled heaps.

"Don't your Mum ever clean up?" asked Amanda, wrinkling her nose in disgust.

"What's the point?" Mark replied, "It would only get dirty again."

A huge television stood in one corner and a music centre in another. Craig switched on the music centre and the sounds of heavy metal rock music blared from the speakers so loudly that the walls vibrated. The sound hurt their ears and they had to shout to make themselves heard, but Craig wouldn't turn it down – he had a reputation to keep up. The neighbours expected them to make a noise and he wasn't going to disappoint them.

Eventually Wendy, hands over her ears, screamed out, "Turn the bloody sound down!" Craig didn't move so she went over and turned the volume control to its lowest level.

Amanda whispered in Craig's ear and took hold of his hand. "Stay down here, you two," he ordered, then he and Amanda took themselves off upstairs.

Mark sniggered and Wendy shrugged her shoulders.

"You know what they're going to do, don't you?"

Wendy stood up. "Give us a fag," she said.

"Well?"

"Well what?"

"You know what they're going to do?"

"Who cares? Give us a fag."

Mark fumbled in his pocket. "So, why can't we? You're my girlfriend after all."

He threw the packet to her, and as she put a cigarette in her mouth she said, "Because I don't want to, that's why – matches!"

He threw the matches across to her. He still thought that if he was nice to her she would let him do something, even if it was only a feel or a look. The trouble was, he didn't know what being nice meant, and although he knew her stepdad was trying it on, he had absolutely no idea how that made her feel. She lit the cigarette and threw the packet and the matches back to him.

"Get one thing straight," she added, "I'm not your girlfriend." She took a deep pull on the cigarette and blew the smoke into the air. She heard the bed creak in the room above them and glanced at the ceiling. "Come on," she snapped, "let's go out."

Upstairs, Craig and Amanda were lying on the bed in a state of disarray. Despite his bravado, Craig was too scared to go all the way even though she was egging him on. They were kissing and touching each other but she wanted to do it.

"Come on," she urged, "let's get undressed and do it properly."

"Don't be daft," he retorted, "what if you have a baby?"

"You can't the first time. I heard my mum say so the other day." Craig digested this bit of information in silence. He had heard that too, but he was still scared. Amanda climbed off the bed and took the rest of her clothes off. It was the first time Craig had seen a completely naked girl and his excitement quickly overruled his fear so that he too shed the remainder of his clothes. His excitement, unfortunately, was short lived. As he moved his body between her legs, he lost control of himself and his first attempt at the sex act was all over before he had a chance to do anything. Amanda was disappointed and wondered if all boys were as quick as that.

"Give us your hanky," she said sulkily. He was embarrassed but he threw his hanky to her and she wiped herself. To cover his embarrassment he snapped, "Come on, let's go out." They both dressed, he quickly and she reluctantly.

'There will be other times,' she thought, 'but will it always be like that, him coming quick before I even get started!'

CHAPTER 6

Tracy Devlin was twelve years old and lived on the Edgetown Estate. A pretty girl with a bubbly personality, she was very bright and attended the school in the village of Southbridge. She liked all the things that girls of her age usually liked – music, disco dancing, fashion clothes, and the company of other girls. There was also an occasional boyfriend, but nothing serious. As a general rule she considered boys of her age to be show-offs and she was not impressed with their antics.

It was Friday, and leaving her friends at the school gates with the promise that she would be going to the disco that evening, she began to cycle the two and a quarter miles home. She had gone about a mile when there was a popping sound and the front tyre went flat, making steering almost impossible.

"Damn," she said loudly, "a puncture. That's all I need." Briefly she wondered whether to walk the rest of the way home or go back to the village and phone home for help. Deciding on the latter course of action she headed back the way she had come. There were no houses on this stretch of the road, just woodland. She was not unduly worried about the loneliness and was more anxious about the prospect of missing the disco. Her parents were strict and would insist that she finished her homework before she went out dancing.

As she trudged wearily back, it was still very hot. She became aware of rustling noises coming from the wood nearby. She paused and peered into the trees, wondering if she might see a fox or maybe a badger, but the sound had stopped and she saw nothing. She continued walking and the noise started again. Something was moving in the undergrowth at the edge of the wood. She was beginning to feel scared. There was another noise, louder this time. She opened her mouth to scream, but before she could do so she was grabbed from behind and a cloth with a strange sweetish smell put roughly over her face. Dropping the bicycle, she kicked out behind and began to pull at the arms that held her. Out of the corner of her eye she thought she glimpsed the face of a clown. The grip tightened and she was pulled back against the body of her assailant. Struggling became difficult as dizziness started and she felt as though she were falling. Pins and needles seemed to envelope her. The world went black and without warning she went limp.

At five o'clock her parents began to get worried. She was always home on time and they knew if there was a problem she would always phone. Her father got into the car and drove to the school, while her mother telephoned all Tracey's friends. When Mr Devlin returned without Tracy, they phoned the hospital. Having got a negative response there, their next step was to drive into town, by now in a state of panic, and go to the police station.

They answered all the questions, supplied a recent photograph, and assured the police that there were no problems at home, no problems with boyfriends, no problems at school, and in fact, no problems at all. They were advised to return home in case Tracy contacted them.

That evening both radio and local television news carried the story of the missing girl. The following morning the police appealed for volunteers and launched a thorough search of the area that surrounded the route she would have taken. The search continued for three days. Hundreds of volunteers turned up, including Jack Templeton, Charlie Slater and his sister Lucy, Phil

Ormisher, the chief mechanic at Charlie's showroom, and Ronnie Thompson, the traffic warden from Jack's department. They searched the wooded areas south of the river from Temsley to Southbridge and then extended the search south of that village.

Inspector Burgess organised house to house enquiries in the village of Southfield but failed to turn up anything that would help them to find the missing girl. No one had seen anything out of the ordinary. Some of the villagers knew Tracy as a friend of their daughter's, but those that saw her that day said she went off on her cycle towards Temsley as she usually did.

Questioning some of the children at the school brought reports of a white van on the outskirts of the village at the time the children came out of school. Following a police appeal, the owner of a white van came forward. He explained that he had broken down and was waiting for the RAC to come and tow him to the nearest garage. After checking his story, he was eliminated from the enquiry. The police were at a loss. Tracy Devlin had vanished from the face of the earth and there was not one single clue to give any indication as to what might have happened.

When Tracy regained consciousness, she found herself lying on a bed in a small room. At the far end was a blackboard, and a table with a chair behind it. In front of that stood a school desk and a chair. It reminded her of a classroom. There were cameras and lights as though someone were making a film. Her head ached and her throat was dry. She struggled to sit up on the bed but her arms and legs were tied. As she pulled at the cords, the door of the room opened and three men came in. All were wearing masks and one was dressed as a teacher, complete with gown and mortarboard. He came across and untied her feet while the other two men went to the cameras.

Pulling her to her feet he led her towards the desk at the front. Nodding to the cameraman he began to speak. "You have been a naughty girl," he droned, "and naughty girls are punished." He opened a drawer in the table and pulled out a cane. Her eyes opened in horror and she began to cry. Fear swept over her and she was unable to speak, then she wet herself. The teacher banged the cane down on the desk. "Disgraceful," he hissed. Then he unzipped her skirt and let it fall to the floor.

She was led over to the table where the second man, who was standing on the other side, leaned forward and pulled on the ropes that secured her arms, forcing her across the table. She felt her pants being pulled down, and twisting her head as she struggled, she caught a glimpse of a small shield tattooed on the inside of a wrist as the sleeve of a dark blue jacket rode up before the first stroke of the cane landed. She closed her eyes tight, screamed and struggled to get free, but the cane hissed through the air again and landed with a crack. The pain was intense. The camera whirred.

The beating stopped and for a moment there was silence, then a rustling sound. She turned her head again and saw the shield once more. The teacher was loosening his trousers.

"No!" she screamed, "Please, no." She felt him move behind her and she screamed again.

Four days after her disappearance, at eleven thirty at night, Janet Mason was returning home. As her car swept round a bend on the Southbridge Road the headlights picked out what looked like a bicycle. Thinking there might have been an accident she stopped and reversed back. She got out of the car walked over to where it lay. It was a girl's cycle and next to it was what looked to be a schoolbag, books strewing out of it. A few feet away lay the naked body of a young girl. She rushed back to the car, grabbed her mobile phone and called the police, asking them to send an ambulance as well.

The police arrived in less than four minutes. As they pulled up, the siren of the ambulance could also be heard coming nearer. Janet showed them where the girl lay. The officer felt for a pulse. "She's still alive," he called out and started to undo the ropes that bound her. The ambulance came to a stop and as the medics came over he left the spot and spoke into his radio.

"It's Tracy Devlin," he reported. "She's still alive."

Superintendent Roy Marks was in charge of the investigation but, despite the extensive enquiries made and the efforts of his team, they had been no nearer finding her after three days than they had from day one. The papers and local television news both came up with the theory that a paedophile ring could be operating in the area, although there was no evidence to support it. Finding Tracy alive was a blessing, not only for her parents, but for all concerned. Since her disappearance, all local children were being vigorously supervised by their parents, but as the police well knew, if there were no further cases, the memory of what happened to Tracy Devlin would soon fade in everyone's mind.

Everyone's that is, except Tracy's. She would not talk about what had happened to her, in fact she would not talk at all. She just sat and stared into space and retreated into a world where the things that she had experienced hadn't happened, could never happen. Her parents were told that she would probably come through it, although there was no guarantee, but it would be a long job.

Jack heard the reports about finding the girl and although he was happy she was alive, he was naturally incensed at the things that had likely been done to her. He discussed it with Lucy and Charlie as they sat in the kitchen after eating their evening meal.

"Something should be done about people who do that sort of thing," commented Lucy angrily.

"It is," replied Jack, "when they catch them."

Charlie shook his head. "What do they do, Jack? Lock them up, that's what they do. Bastards like that should be castrated."

Jack looked at them both, his mind racing. Tracy Devlin's dreadful experience was the thing that finally made up his mind. He lit up a cigarette, drew deeply and whispered, "Justice does seem to be sadly lacking. I think it needs a helping hand." He stood up and collected the empty plates. "By the way, Charlie, two drug addicts have been arrested for the job on your house. It was their fingerprints the police found."

Charlie sat up at this news. "Do you think you could find out when they're going to be released? A few broken bones are in order as far as I'm concerned."

"Sorry, Charlie, someone beat you to it. The pair of them have already had both their arms broken plus a few other things. Anyway, I hear they'll be in prison for quite a while yet."

"Who did that to them? I'll buy him a drink."

"I don't think you will. The police aren't one hundred per cent sure, but it's a good bet that Bannerman was the bloke who almost certainly put your alarm out of action and enabled those thugs to get in."

"So maybe we should do something about *him*," declared Charlie.

"Maybe," mused Jack.

"Well, we've got to do something, Jack." Charlie's frustration was evident in his voice. "The police are either unable or unwilling to do much and the government seems to be running scared of human rights activists and European law."

Jack then disclosed the episode of Ronnie Thompson and Dave Turner and when he had finished he declared, "I know he'll sign up and that will make four of us." Lighting another cigarette he smiled grimly and added, "Between us we should be able to do something."

"Five," corrected Charlie. "Phil Ormisher, my mechanic, has suggested that he's willing to lend a hand too."

Jack nodded. 'Things are looking up,' he thought. 'Or are they?'

CHAPTER 7

John Bannerman had been mad as hell when the house he was planning to burgle four weeks earlier had been taken over by the two druggies. Earlier in the day he had seen to it that the alarm would not go off, and as always, he didn't hang around. When he had returned to finish off the job, he'd heard the two men smashing the place up, looked through a window and recognised them. He made a hasty retreat as, for all he knew, someone might already have called the police – the idiots had been making enough noise to wake the dead.

He knew he would have to do something about them and, Bannerman being Bannerman, had made sure less than two weeks later that they would not be treading on his toes again, at least not for a while. They didn't know who had put them in hospital, so could not come after him, and anyway they would be incapable of causing any more destruction for a long time to come. Having both arms broken, to say nothing of the other injuries they received, would be a bit of a handicap. Bannerman had also heard that the two had been arrested by the police for the burglary as well, as their fingerprints were found everywhere.

All this had made Bannerman feel a lot happier. Wielding a crow bar on those two drugged-up slobs had given him a lot of satisfaction and set the adrenaline flowing, making him feel powerful. He had just left Beaky Williams at the Windmill pub, having collected five hundred pounds for goods supplied – other people's goods of course. They always used the Windmill pub on a Saturday evening because, owing to its reputation, it was never very busy and they could conduct their business in relative privacy. When he left there and walked back to his car, he had actually been humming to himself.

It was July and there had been no let-up in the hot weather. Even though it was dark it was still very warm. The day had been hot and the evening was heavy and oppressive. There was just the slightest breeze as he walked across the unlit and almost deserted car park to where his new red BMW was parked. As he reached the car he paused to light a cigarette. The lighter clicked and the flame flared in the darkness, lighting up his smooth features. He was twenty-five years old, six foot tall and very slim, not to say skinny, giving him the appearance of being undernourished. His hair was jet black and looked perpetually greasy. A few strands usually hung in front of his eyes and he was continually brushing them back with his fingers. His eyes seemed to be black holes in his face and his heavy eyelids looked as though they were always half closed. The clothes he wore were casual, with the exception of his shoes, which were black and highly polished. Gleaming black shoes was an obsession, one of life's essentials to Bannerman. He was, in a strange way, quite good looking and never short of girlfriends. Tonight, though, he had had business to deal with, so tonight he was alone.

As he snapped the lighter shut another light burned through the darkness, a torch beam. He turned towards the light but it lifted and shone full in his face. Raising his hand to shield his eyes he turned his head to one side in an effort to see beyond the light. He could just make out two figures.

A voice with a Scottish lilt broke the silence. "Hello, John. Smoking is bad for your health. Didn't you know?"

Bannerman was not amused. "Who the fuck are you and what do you want?"

"Police," came the reply, "and we would like a few words."

A warrant card appeared and wavered in and out of the torch beam. Bannerman drew deeply on the cigarette in his mouth and drew in a lungful of smoke. He blew it out slowly into the night air. "If you bastards want to talk to me then I want my brief." He replaced the cigarette between his lips and turned towards his car. A hand reached out and snatched the cigarette away, pulling the skin off his lips.

"Fuck you," he cried. A boot crashed between his legs and with a gasp of pain he doubled up and collapsed in an untidy heap on the ground.

As he lay there, one of the officers went through his pockets removing his car keys, wallet, and the bundle of ten-pound notes he had just received from Beaky Williams. He was dragged to his feet, his hands forced behind his back and handcuffs snapped into place as a white police van pulled slowly and almost silently into the car park. The rear door opened and Bannerman was pushed roughly into the back. Two officers climbed in with him and the rear door slammed shut. The van drove slowly out of the car park and turned left onto the main road.

As the pain in his groin subsided and he could breathe more easily, Bannerman looked up at the two officers. One of them looked quite old and had a moustache. The other one wore spectacles and had a scar running down the side of his face. Scarface looked down at him. When he spoke, Bannerman recognised the Scottish burr.

"Back with us, are you? We told you smoking was bad for your health."

Bannerman heaved himself into a sitting position. "Listen to me, you scotch git – " the rest of the sentence was cut off as a fist smashed into his face, splitting his lip and sending him crashing back down on the floor. He lay there tasting his blood.

"Scotch is a drink, laddie. I am a Scot but definitely not a git."

Bannerman decided that silence was the best policy, at least for the time being. He had never known the police to be this aggressive and he wondered why they were acting this way. Still, he would have these bastards in court the first chance he got, that was certain. Maybe he would even get compensation. He smiled inwardly at that thought.

Soon however, even though he was on the floor of the van and his vision was limited, he knew without doubt that this was not the way to the police station, not from the pub anyway. They passed the hospital on the left so he knew they must be in Mallerton Road. They had come round in a wide circle. He was going to ask why they were going this way but thought better of it. He started to worry when they turned away from the nick into Bridge Street and over the river.

After about fifteen minutes the van turned down a bumpy track and into some trees where it came to a halt. The rear door was opened, he was pulled out and pushed face down on the ground. The scar-faced officer crouched down beside him and put a tape recorder next to his head.

"Now then," came the Scottish drawl, "we will ask you some questions and you will answer them." The machine was switched on. "You are still doing burglaries, aren't you?"

The reply was typical Bannerman despite the treatment he had already received. "Bollocks! I'm saying fuck-all to you." A boot crashed into his side and he screamed out in pain.

"Wrong answer, John. Now, same question. You're still doing burglaries?"

"Yes," he cried, "yes."

"Good. Who takes your stuff?"

He hesitated, saw the boot move backwards and decided it was in his best interests to talk.

"Beaky Williams," he said quickly. "He takes all my stuff."

"Address?"

"Number 7 Jackson Close on the Eastleigh Estate. He keeps it all in his garage."

"We want to know about Mrs Lawson."

Bannerman was puzzled at this question and stumbled over his answer. "I … er … don't know any Mrs Lawson."

Scarface grabbed his hair and pulled his head backwards.

"Yes you do, you bastard, you put her in hospital. An eighty-year-old lady who couldn't possibly do you any harm, yet you broke her arm and blacked her eyes." The grip on his hair tightened and he winced. "Then you had the cheek to draw her pension."

Bannerman remembered. "I only pushed her out of the way," he whined, "and I never drew her pension. Beaky's wife Ginny does that whenever I get a book."

"Oh, well," said Scarface, "that makes it all right then, doesn't it?" He slammed Bannerman's face back onto the ground. "We know you haven't got a bank account so where do you keep your ill-gotten gains?"

"I told you – Beaky Williams."

"Your money, John, your cash, WHERE IS IT?" He hesitated too long and the boot crashed into his side once more. The pain was excruciating. "I don't mind kicking you all night, you thieving wee bastard, but is it worth the pain?"

He most definitely didn't want to tell them about his money but the pain was too much for him so he started talking.

While they were having this friendly conversation,

Bannerman's BMW pulled into the clearing. Scarface finally switched off the tape recorder, crossed to where the car stood and spoke very quietly to the driver. It was Phil Ormisher.

"Take Bannerman to his flat and pick up all his cash. He'll tell you where it is. But search the place and see what else you can find. Then bring him back here. Ronnie will go with you."

Still handcuffed, Bannerman was bundled into the back seat of his own car with another officer for company and driven to his flat in Riverside Lane. The flats where he lived were the most expensive as they overlooked the river from the front, a wide expanse of the embankment from the side and a recreation ground at the rear. They also had security doors to stop any undesirables from gaining access.

The driver parked the car carefully away from a street light outside the block opposite the children's playground. Helping Bannerman out of the car, all three walked down the path, opened the security door and disappeared inside. Bannerman had finally realised these were not the police he was dealing with. Or if they were, they were as bent as he was crooked. More than once he had thought of shouting out to raise the alarm, but would anyone believe his claims that his escorts were not the police? Anyway, what would the consequences of such an action be? No, he would just have to bide his time and see what happened.

Half an hour later the three emerged and walked back to the car. One of the officers carried a medium-size suitcase. The BMW reversed back to the main road and drove quietly back the way it had come.

Driving over the bridge away from the town and into the darkness, Bannerman was hoping his ordeal was over. They had all his money and a pile of other things. If they were the police, they could hardly take him to the police station and charge him with burglary or assault. Besides, they weren't going to the nick so they would probably leave him in the woods. Alas for him, he was mistaken. His ordeal was only just beginning and it would last for a very long time.

When they arrived back in the clearing he was dragged from the car and forced face down on the ground once more. Ronnie took the case over to the van and speaking quietly, opened it.

"There must be sixty thousand pounds here plus credit cards, driving licences, passports, and other goodies." The case was snapped shut again. Bannerman tried to see what was happening but was unable to lift his head high enough. Suddenly, Scarface, was back again, his Scottish accent more pronounced.

"Now then, John, we're going to do you a favour. You'd like that, wouldn't you?" He nodded confirmation even though he didn't know what the favour was going to be. Hands pulled him into a sitting position and the handcuffs were unfastened. Relief flooded through him but it was short lived. The handcuffs were fastened again with his hands in front of him. He was then pushed face down with his arms stretched up over his head.

"We are going to stop you thieving, John." The voice was amiable, friendly, a sort of everybody's-favourite-uncle voice. "You would like to stop thieving, wouldn't you?" Before he could answer, a gag was fastened round his mouth and pulled tight, but he still managed to nod. "That's good, because if we catch you thieving again," there was an ominous pause, "well, we won't think about that, eh?"

He heard the van door slam shut and a pair of shiny black boots appeared in front of his face. The knees bent and a hand pulled his head upwards. He was looking into the face of the man with the moustache, whose other hand held a small sledgehammer. Fear invaded every cell in his body and he tried to struggle and shout out, but it was no use.

A voice drifted over to him. "This is lesson one, John." He turned his head sideways so that he could see. His arms were held down and he knew exactly what the hammer was for. They were going to break his hand.

'Oh no,' he tried to say, 'not that, please,' but there were only muffled sounds from beneath his gag. Warmth flooded his groin as fear emptied his bladder. One of the group, maybe the hammer man, started to hum a tune and he found himself stupidly trying to remember where he had heard it before. He closed his eyes and clenched his fists as the hammer was raised but it made no difference whatsoever as it smashed down on his left hand breaking all the bones. He tried to scream as the bones of his fingers cut through his skin, but he failed. He was mercifully unconscious as the hammer travelled downwards the second time, on its journey to his right hand.

At two-thirty the following morning, Ruth Machin was travelling home. She was a very happy lady having spent an unforgettable day and most of the night with her boyfriend. Driving round the ring road she thought back over the last few hours, reliving the excitement. Something caught her eye. She was approaching the 'Goalkeeper', a name that the local populace had given to a strange wooden statue of a man standing between two posts. What it was supposed to represent was known only to its maker, although there had been various suggestions, usually about the local football team, and usually very uncomplimentary.

Ruth slowed down and put the headlights on full beam. She could see the figure of a man sitting on the ground and leaning, or rather propped up, against one of the posts. She stopped, got out and moved nearer. He had been beaten about the face and she could see that he was actually tied to the post. There was a large white card round his neck, which was probably what had caught her eye in the first place, and on it was written in large black letters,

I AM A BURGLAR AND I BEAT UP OLD LADIES
THIS IS LESSON 1

She read the card and looked down at his hands, thinking he was holding something white. As she looked closer she was horrified to realise that bones were sticking right through the flesh. She stifled a scream but could not stop herself from vomiting at the sight. Staggering back to the car she pulled a mobile phone from her handbag and dialled 999. She asked for the police and an ambulance, gave her location and then sat in the car wondering which one would turn up first.

Just after two-thirty in the morning, Andy Mills was pacing the floor of his living room clutching a small glass of sherry. He did this when he couldn't sleep, which was more often than not just lately. He switched on the scanner that stood next to his music centre, eased his more-than-ample frame into his favourite armchair and began to listen to the local police broadcasts. As a journalist Andy found this pastime very rewarding on occasions, even if it was illegal.

He had been in the newspaper business ever since leaving school at the age of fifteen, forty-eight years earlier. He had worked on the *Temsley Gazette* for the past twenty years having moved up from London to get out of the 'rat race' that had become the norm on the national papers. In two years' time he would retire from the *Gazette*, something he wasn't looking forward to. Newspapers were in his blood, so to speak, and he just could not visualise a retirement without the hustle and bustle of office life and the need to keep to deadlines.

As he sipped at his sherry he heard a request that someone attend the 'Goalkeeper' where an injured man had been found. An ambulance was on its way. He sipped the sherry again. An injured man attracted only half his attention until he heard the name John Bannerman. As a local reporter he knew that name very well. His interest increased further when he heard that Bannerman had had his hands broken and that there was a notice round his neck declaring that he was a burglar who beat up old ladies. So this was not a road accident, as he had at first thought, nor even the result of a brawl. This was something much more interesting. This was what – payback day, perhaps, for someone Bannerman had robbed? Maybe it was vigilantes. He decided to go to the hospital and see what he could find out.

At the hospital he told a weary-looking nurse that his name was Bannerman and that his son had been brought in earlier. She looked at him with some sympathy and just a hint of puzzlement. She stared at him as though she were trying to decide whether this man could really be the father of the young man currently anaesthetised on an operating table. Finally, giving him the benefit of the doubt, she told him as much as she knew.

"He's in deep shock," she informed him. "He has broken ribs, severe bruising to the face and body, and both his hands are severely damaged with a number of fingers broken." She paused as though waiting for a response. Andy stayed silent but managed to look shocked at the news.

"He has been to X-ray and is now in theatre. I suggest you phone in the morning."

Andy continued to look shocked and whispered, "His injuries are not life-threatening, are they?"

The nurse smiled. "No, they're not," she assured him, "but he has had a rather bad time."

Andy nodded, and as he watched her walk away he was thinking not about the trim figure of the nurse but of Bannerman's injuries, and his thought was, 'Serves the bastard right.'

CHAPTER 8

When Inspector Burgess arrived at the CID office at six o'clock that morning there was a message informing him of what had happened to John Bannerman and instructing him to look into it. A wry smile flickered across his face as he thought how strange the way things could turn out. It had been his intention to bring in Bannerman that day for questioning about the ransacking of Charlie Slater's house and the assault on the two drug addicts, Green and Tyler, both of whom had been charged with the burglary. He knew that Bannerman had nothing to do with the Slater break-in as Green and Tyler had left their fingerprints everywhere, but the method of disabling the alarm had Bannerman's signature all over it. There was also no doubt that he had been responsible for the beating given to them, but he knew deep down he had as much chance of proving that as he had of winning the lottery. In fact he probably had more chance of winning the lottery.

Sitting at his desk he switched on the computer, more from habit than because he would use it, and while it bleeped and buzzed he reflected on the changes he had seen in the thirty-five years he had been in the force. Back then he had been a nineteen-year-old full of enthusiasm and eager to succeed in his chosen career. The job became his life. He married and had two children, but the marriage failed because his job always seemed to come first and his wife turned to another man for the love and affection she craved. Now at fifty-four, slightly underweight, going grey at the temples and living alone, his enthusiasm had diminished but not disappeared. He sometimes wondered what life would be like if his marriage had held together, but he never dwelt on those thoughts for long. Sometimes he blamed Margaret for not being more understanding, but mostly he blamed himself for the same offence. Deciding it was too early to go to the hospital or to Ruth Machin's house, he busied himself with the paperwork on the cases he was currently looking into. Being Sunday meant there were few distractions at the station and he would be able to bring everything up to date. He was still doing paperwork when the Chief Inspector, Dave Cross, put his head round the door.

"'Morning, Colin."

He looked up, surprised to see him but managing to conceal it. Sundays for the DCI usually meant the golf course. "'Morning, Dave."

"I see you will be looking into the Bannerman incident today."

"Yes." He wondered what was coming and thought, 'I bet he tells me to take one of the new starters with me.'

"Take DC Tate with you. Needs a bit of experience, you know."

"You mean WDC Jenny Tate?"

"Yes, that's her, but don't call her a WDC, she doesn't like the 'woman' tag on the rank."

This time Colin was surprised and raised his eyebrows quizzically.

Dave Cross saw the look and added, "Something to do with being sexist – you know what I mean." Colin did know, but before he could make a reply the Chief Inspector instructed, "Keep me up to date on it," shut the door and was gone, leaving Colin wondering what working with a WDC, who didn't like to be called a woman, would be like. He thought about his retirement. Only a year to go now, then he wouldn't have to worry about funny women, only his garden.

He knew Jenny Tate of course, or rather he knew what she looked like. Good looking girl he remembered, mid-twenties, tall, five ten, slim with curves and bumps in all the right places. Her dark hair was cut short and she had deep intelligent eyes. She always had a serious look about her and he found himself wondering if she had a sense of humour. He wasn't happy about taking new arrivals with him under normal circumstances and a women's rights activist without a sense of humour would be just the icing to cover his cake of misery.

He continued with the paperwork and at ten o'clock went to the canteen for a cup of tea. As he passed the main CID office he stuck his head in and told the sergeant to tell WDC Tate to be in the back yard with a car at half past ten. In the canteen he found that the smell of frying was too much to resist, so he had a bacon sandwich with his tea before making his way down to the back yard. It was nearly twenty minutes to eleven when he walked across the compound to where she was waiting by the car.

She was as attractive as he had remembered, and then some. The clothes she wore were plain and simple but fitted her perfectly. Their lack of colour seemed to accentuate her air of seriousness.

"'Morning, sir." He noticed with some envy her even white teeth as she spoke.

"'Morning," he replied. "Let's go to the hospital and hear what Bannerman has to say. I don't like him or his activities but I hate paperwork even more." She seemed to brighten up at this piece of news, making Colin wonder if he had misjudged her.

A doctor at the hospital told them the extent of Bannerman's injuries.

"Sounds like he could be out of a job," remarked Colin, "if his hands are as bad as that."

"What was he?" asked the doctor curiously. "A watchmaker or something?"

"No," replied the policeman, "he was a burglar! When can we see him?"

"Now if you want, but don't stay too long, he's still groggy from the anaesthetic."

On the way to the ward Jenny Tate questioned, "Was it wise to tell the doctor Bannerman was a burglar?"

"Probably not, Constable, but he is still a burglar and a rose by any other name smells just as sweet … or something like that anyway."

Bannerman was in a side ward all by himself. He looked terrible. His face was bruised and cut, his eyes were black and puffy, and both hands were covered with white bandages.

"Who did this to you, John?"

Bannerman looked up and mumbled painfully through swollen lips. "The police."

Colin was startled at the answer. "The police? Pull the other one, John, it's got bells on it."

With difficulty, Bannerman related what had happened the previous evening, leaving out the bit about Beaky Williams, Ginny, and Mrs Lawson's pension book.

"How do you know they were police?" asked Jenny Tate.

"You what!" It hurt him to talk but he carried on. "I'm not fucking blind. Three wore police uniforms and the one in plain clothes showed me his warrant card. They carried police radios and drove a police van. To my mind that makes them coppers."

"They could have been in fancy dress."

"Yeah, well, I wouldn't know about that, would I?"

"What were their shoulder numbers?"

"Dunno, didn't see them."

"What about the van's registration number?"

"Didn't see that neither."

"Didn't see much at all did you, John?"

Bannerman nodded towards his heavily bandaged hands. "I saw a bloody great sledgehammer wielded by some little scotch git in a copper's uniform. He was humming a bleeding tune when he done it too."

"What tune was that then, John?"

"I don't bloody well know, do I? Just some poncey tune."

"We'll come and talk to you again, John, we have to have a statement from you. Meanwhile, if you think of anything just call the officer who will be waiting outside."

As they left, Bannerman managed to shout. "Bastards!"

Colin turned to Jenny. "He must have known my mother."

She said nothing. She was still trying to decide whether she liked this sarcastic officer who hated paperwork. She wondered how much more of the police work he hated.

Back at the car he gave her the address of Ruth Machin and they drove round to see her.

On the journey she asked, "Do you believe him, sir, about the police doing it?"

Colin looked mildly surprised. "Believe him? No. I know practically everyone in the force, not just at Church Street, and I can't think of anyone who would do a thing like that." He thought for moment. "Mind you, he wouldn't have gone with them if he didn't think they were police. The police wouldn't have trouble picking him up but anyone else would. He's a vicious bastard."

Ruth Machin was at home padding around in her dressing-gown. She invited them in and apologised for her state of dress.

"A very late night," she explained.

They had no trouble getting a statement from her about what had happened the previous evening, or rather earlier that morning, but unfortunately there was nothing in it that could shed any light as to who was responsible for the state that Bannerman was now in. It was with an air of failure that they made their way back to the station.

Back at the office Colin opened a file headed 'Bannerman' and placed all the information he had about the incident, which was precious little, inside it.

"From what Bannerman said, do you think you could find the place where he was taken?"

Jenny put her head on one side as she considered the question, and nodded. "Yes, I'm sure I could."

Colin dropped the file in his drawer. "Right then, let's go."

As they were about to leave the office a uniformed constable came and put a packet on the desk.

"This was in the post-box, sir. Hand-delivered, by the looks of it."

Colin looked at the package, saw there were no stamps, and dropped it in the drawer with the Bannerman file.

"I'll open it when we get back."

After one or two false starts they managed to find a place that was pretty much as Bannerman described. There was little evidence of any disturbance except some vague tyre tracks, but Colin noticed something on the ground that looked suspiciously like blood. He scooped it up and dropped it in a plastic bag which he pulled from his inside pocket. "You never know," he said, "this might be Bannerman's blood. If it is, we'll get a few people down here for a fingertip search." Glancing round he added, "Although I doubt if they'll find anything."

As they drove back into town once more, Colin turned to his young colleague. "Well, Detective Constable Tate, any ideas on the Bannerman incident yet?"

Jenny Tate was full of ideas and proceeded to voice them. "It's obviously vigilantes, sir, but whether it's just Bannerman they've picked on we won't know unless it happens again."

"Why do you say it's *obviously* vigilantes?"

"The notice round his neck, I don't think anyone but vigilantes would have left such a thing. It's a statement of things to come."

"Like H G Wells you mean?"

"Pardon?"

"Nothing, forget it." He pondered on what she had said. She had voiced his thoughts as though she could read his mind. There couldn't really be any other explanation, but the thought of a group of nutters taking the law into their own hands and breaking bones with sledgehammers wasn't something he cared to think about.

CHAPTER 9

At Church Street he sent Jenny off for some lunch and took the Bannerman file from the drawer. The bulky envelope that had arrived earlier stared up at him. He opened it and tipped the contents out on the desk. There were a number of driving licences and credit cards in various names, plus two passports and a photograph of Bannerman leaning against the 'Goalkeeper' with the white card round his neck. There was also a typed statement which gave the dates, times, and addresses of several recent burglaries, including Mrs Lawson's, that Bannerman had admitted to. It also advised that Beaky and Ginny Williams had a garage full of stolen goods and a house full of pension books and various other goodies that Bannerman, among others, had supplied to them. As he read the statement, Jenny Tate came back into the office. When he had finished, he handed it to her.

"It looks like you might be right, Constable."

He went to the Chief Inspector's office to update him and arrange for a search warrant for the Williams' address.

Both garage and house proved to be an Aladdin's cave of stolen goods, many of which would be readily identified. Gerald Williams, known to everyone as Beaky because of his very long nose, and his wife Ginny, were arrested and taken to the station for questioning where they were put in separate rooms. Neither, was inclined to be cooperative. Beaky refused to say a word except for demanding a solicitor.

Ginny started out the same way, but when Colin told her that unless she started to talk he would be forced to charge her with burglary and the assault on Mrs Lawson, she yelled, "Oh no, I never did that!"

"The pension book says you did. It's got your fingerprints all over it and we have a statement saying that a woman fitting your description cashed it." He pulled out a packet of Polo mints, popped one in his mouth and added, "A handwriting expert could no doubt prove that you filled it in too."

Ginny Williams glared at him through her small eyes, now just slits in her face. "I didn't do it," she snarled, "and you can't make me say I did."

Colin raised his eyebrows and looked at the woman opposite him as she shifted in her chair, trying to make herself more comfortable. She was a short skinny woman with straggly blonde hair that hung down to her shoulders. Her face had a pinched look with a wide mouth that was covered in the gaudiest, thickest red lipstick he had ever seen on a woman. She stared back at him defiantly, brushed the hair from her face with her fingers then pulled out a packet of cigarettes from her dress pocket and lit one.

"What's the going rate for burglary with assault, Constable, plus of course fraudulently cashing a pension? Five years, or is it seven?"

Jenny took the hint. "Definitely seven, Guv."

He stood up and said, "Interview terminated at 16:10 hours." Then he switched off the tape. "Right, charge her and lock her up. Pity she didn't co-operate, she might have got a lighter sentence."

He opened the door as if to leave and Ginny called out, "Wait."

He closed the door again. "All right," she shouted, "but just you remember, I'm co-operating." Colin switched the machine back on and she started to tell him about Bannerman and a few others that Beaky had bought 'goods' from.

Inspector Burgess and Jenny Tate made a few arrests that evening and the clear-up rate of burglaries showed a significant improvement. Jenny was pleased with her first day's work with her new boss but Colin thought only of all the extra paperwork involved.

Just before he decided to go home he was called to see the senior officer, Superintendent Marks, and give him a progress report first-hand. Superintendent Marks was a strange person in that no one could ever remember hearing him laugh. He was known as Groucho to all the staff, not just because of his name, but because he always had something to moan about. Despite that, he was considered to be a 'good copper' who was up to date with all the latest information on law and procedure – and like all the superintendents that Colin had worked under, he was a stickler for procedure. Everything had to be done 'by the book'.

Colin gave him all the available evidence about the attack, which didn't amount to much, and a brief outline of what Bannerman had told him. Marks listened without interruption except for the occasional 'Hmm' and 'I see', and when Colin was finished he said, "So, we have four men," he held up four fingers, "three in uniform," he put a finger down, "one with a warrant card," he put two more fingers down, "and all with radios driving a police van." Placing his elbows on the desk, he steepled his fingers and continued, "One is oldish with a moustache, another wears spectacles and has a scar, and another is possibly a Scot who hums a tune while smashing hands with a sledgehammer."

"That's about it, sir."

Marks nodded his head thoughtfully. "But you have evidence that will convict Bannerman of burglary and assault, plus one or two other villains, and a chance to increase the clear-up rate?"

Colin nodded. "Plus," he added, "we have taken Beaky and Ginny Williams off the streets, which takes the major fence out of circulation."

Marks leaned forward across the desk and lowered his voice. "Are you sure this couldn't have been the work of some of our officers?"

"As certain as I can be, sir. I can't see any of our people doing this sort of thing. There's no doubt in my mind that this is the work of vigilantes."

Marks stared at Colin, shaking his head vigorously. "No, no, we must *not* use the word 'vigilantes', it might trigger more violence. In any case there is no evidence to support that theory."

"With all due respect, sir, the evidence we have all points to vigilante action – the card round his neck, the information to convict, even the injury itself – everything says vigilante."

"Well, *we* won't." Marks stood up and began to wave his hands about as he spoke. "It will be some sort of grudge," he insisted, "that one villain has against another." He put a finger in the collar of his shirt and moved it as though easing the tightness. "Vigilantes, Inspector, is not an option. Is that understood?"

"Perfectly, sir, but what about the local paper?"

Marks ignored the question and instead said, "I hear you're a bit of a gardener."

Colin was taken aback. Marks was not known for showing interest in his officers' social lives. "Just a bit, sir," he replied, trying to sound suitably modest.

"Well, I suggest you do some more digging." He leaned forward. "I don't want vigilantes on the streets of Temsley and I don't want talk of them either."

He sat back down and Colin, a bit put out at the sarcasm, knew the interview was at an end.

On Monday morning, Andy Mills at the *Temsley Gazette* received a similar envelope to that which Inspector Burgess had received the day before. It contained photocopies of everything that the Inspector had received, although the names and numbers on the credit cards and driving licences had been obliterated. He took it to his editor and copied the contents, thinking that he might have to hand over the documents to the police as evidence. Having discussed the matter, he went to the police station to see whoever was in charge of the Bannerman case. He was told that Inspector Burgess was dealing with the case but that he was at present unavailable. He tried twice more during the day and on the third attempt he was told that the Inspector was in.

Andy Mills was no stranger to Colin Burgess, and on being informed that he was downstairs waiting to see him with regard to some evidence he had, he had a strong feeling it would be about Bannerman. He went down to the enquiry desk and escorted Andy back to his office, watching with some amusement as Andy tried to make himself comfortable on a chair not designed for one of his size. He noticed the bald patch, which was new, and the thick horn-rimmed glasses that he always wore. They reminded him of the children's television programme 'Joe Ninety'. He was smartly turned out as always, but the suit he always wore was well worn, as were the brown brogues on his feet, making Colin wonder if they were the only articles of clothing the elderly reporter possessed.

"What can I do for you, Andy?"

The reporter looked at Colin through half closed eyes and smiled. "Very good, Colin, I'm impressed."

The policeman let a questioning look settle on his face but said nothing.

"I'm here to ask about Bannerman. In hospital, as I understand?"

Colin nodded. "Yes, he had an argument with a rival, we think."

"Try 'vigilantes', Colin," Andy said with an air of satisfaction. Self-assured, he took out the envelope and emptied the contents on the desk, Colin recognised it as similar to the one he himself had received the day before. "This makes very interesting reading and the photograph is very good. You can see every word on the white card as clear as day." There was no hesitation or pause when he said again, "It *is* vigilantes."

"That's not how we see it."

"That's not how Marks sees it, you mean." He put his hands on the arms of the chair and pulled himself forward. "Come on, Colin, the man has three broken ribs, severe bruising and smashed hands."

"You're very well informed about something that isn't public knowledge yet." He pushed his glasses back up his nose.

"I was at the hospital talking to one of the nurses."

"All right, Andy, but this is not official." Burgess proceeded to give him a limited statement based on what Bannerman had said, adding, "If you print anything that jeopardises the case against Bannerman or anyone else, I will find something to charge you with, believe me."

When the reporter had gone, Colin went to the window and gazed out across the backyard. He was inexplicably agitated. Why had the local rag been chosen to publish the story and not the nationals? The only explanation, assuming that the nationals really had not been informed, was that the vigilantes were a local group concerned with local crime, at least for the time being. "Shit," he muttered to himself. "Bloody vigilantes. Why couldn't they have waited until I retired? This is going to be a bloody nightmare." He was well aware that crime was on the increase, and the punishments, when the villains were convicted, were pathetically inadequate. He also knew that the public in general were very unhappy with the situation and that the chances of anyone co-operating with the police and helping them find the vigilantes were slim. In fact, the chances were almost certainly non-existent.

When the newspaper came out the following day the headlines screamed 'VIGILANTES!', and the story told how Bannerman had had his hands broken with a sledgehammer. It made no mention of the fact that the vigilantes were dressed as police officers, but only because it was the one thing that Andy Mills did not know.

CHAPTER 10

On a busy Saturday afternoon in the middle of July the Sharks were at the Northway Retail Park. They hadn't done anything wrong, but the security men in each of the shops were keeping a close eye on them. At some of the stores the uniformed security officers refused them entry. News of their presence at Northway spread rapidly. They had a reputation and no one was taking any chances. They were watched carefully on the in-store cameras and it was made clear to them they were being watched.

A white police van pulled into the park and stopped outside the department store the Sharks had just entered. Four police officers got out and wandered over to the security guard who had been following the gang.

"There are four youths in the area," said one of the officers in a broad Irish accent. "They call themselves the Sharks and we would like a word with them down at the station." The guard nodded toward the store they had just entered.

"They're in there. We're keeping our eyes on them, but if you want, you can go in and get them. It will save us a lot of worry and work." The officer nodded his thanks and motioned for the others to enter the shop.

"Nice and quietly," he said, "we don't want to make a fuss."

The four officers moved soundlessly round the shop and one by one the Sharks were led out to the waiting van. Craig Thomas was the only one to cause a problem. He started shouting and waving his arms around and knocking goods off the shelves, so he was promptly handcuffed and frog-marched out. Shoppers, who were witness to the event, smiled in smug satisfaction thinking that the four youths were shoplifters and had been arrested. Craig continued to shout obscenities and the officer whispered in his ear, "There's a van outside and if you don't shut up you will discover, when we are in it, how easy it would be for me to break your arm while you are resisting arrest. Do you understand?"

Craig went quiet. He didn't believe him about breaking his arm but he decided not to take any chances. When all four were in the van they were handcuffed to the legs of the seats, blindfolded and made to sit on the floor. The van pulled out of the park and turned right. It went across the roundabout into the High Street, turned left into Northfield Road and right into East Street. For a moment the Sharks thought they were being taken home but it drove straight past Bradley Street where they all lived. They began to feel alarmed.

"You bastards," yelled Craig, "you can't do this, we're children. We'll fucking sue you." The blindfolds were lifted and while the other three watched, the officer slapped the boy's face – hard.

"Any more noise and we'll gag you as well." The blindfolds were then replaced.

All the Sharks were scared, but the only one who didn't show it was Wendy. She had learned to hide her fear from her stepfather and she did the same in this situation. She was almost certain that their captors were not policemen. She was sure that they were the vigilantes the newspaper had been on about. It scared her because she wondered if they were all going to have their hands broken by a sledgehammer like the burglar, but she said nothing. Craig had started to cry when he was slapped and Amanda was sniffling and shaking with fright. Mark kept muttering "Oh, bloody hell," and rocking backwards and forwards.

The van crossed the river and headed out of town towards a new, but empty, industrial park. It pulled into a deserted factory unit and the shutters came down with a resounding clank. The blindfolds were removed and the children were herded out of the van into the vastness of the building, empty except for a table and chair to one side and a workbench with two lengths of rope on it. There was another person there too, a blonde-haired woman with a big bust, wearing glasses. She stood at the door to the small office watching and saying nothing. With the exception of Wendy, they were all shocked. They had expected to find themselves in a police station, not in an empty building. They were taken to stand in front of the table. One of the policemen sat down and, opening a notebook, turned to Craig and began to ask questions.

"Name and address." Craig hesitated and then said, "Bollocks, this ain't the police station."

The Irish drawl spoke softly in his ear. "You have a short memory, lad." Craig, a sneer on his face, turned his head towards the voice and was rewarded with another hard slap. He yelled at the shock and then began to cry again.

Turning to Mark, the officer at the table said, "Name and address." Mark didn't hesitate, he was too scared.

"Mark Thomas, 20 Bradley Street, Eastley." There were tears welling up in his eyes as he added, "That's my brother Craig and he lives with me."

"How old are you?"

"Eleven, and he's thirteen," he said quickly.

The officer looked at Amanda who, without waiting to be spoken to said, "Amanda Green, 16 Bradley Street, age thirteen."

There was a pause while the officer wrote in the notebook and then his gaze turned to Wendy.

"Wendy Miles, 6 Bradley Street and I'm twelve." She took a deep breath and asked, "What are you going to do to us? Are you like my stepfather?"

The officer looked intrigued. "What's your stepfather like?"

"He's a bloody pervert and he wants to, you know, do it to me." Her bottom lip started to quiver but she managed to keep control. "Is that what you're going to do?"

The officer wrote something in his notebook and replied, "No, we're nothing like your stepfather." Turning to Craig, who had stopped crying, he said, "Same question again."

Craig wiped his eyes on his sleeve and spoke in a subdued voice. "Craig Thomas, 20 Bradley Street age thirteen."

The officer stood up. "We want to know why you caused the pileup on Mile End Road by dropping bricks on the traffic."

Craig and Mark immediately retorted, "It wasn't us," but before they could say anything else Wendy shouted, "Stop lying, they know it was us."

Amanda started to wail loudly, saying, "I told him we shouldn't have done it. It was his fault." She pointed to Craig. "He made us do it."

"Stop lying," said Wendy again. "You enjoyed it, you even called one of them a yuppie bastard 'cos you thought he had a mobile phone."

Amanda glared at Wendy. "Anyway, you've done it before, we all have."

The officer was somewhat surprised by Wendy's show of honesty. "Why do you do it?" he asked her.

Wendy shrugged her shoulders. "Don't know. It's daring somehow, right? Anyway, when you do things like that, right, the other kids don't start bullying you or anything." She dropped her voice to a whisper. "School's boring." Her voice rose as she added, "and the old man right, he's a bastard."

The officer with the Irish accent placed a sheet of paper on the table. "This says that you were responsible for the traffic collision on Mile End Road by dropping stones on the vehicles. Sign it, all of you." Wendy didn't hesitate, just picked up the pen and signed her name. Amanda signed next and then the two brothers.

"You are now going to be taught a lesson. It is lesson one, so after you leave here I suggest you change your ways. No more truanting and no more vandalism or thieving. If you stick to that you'll be all right. If you don't, well let me say you don't want to know what lesson two is."

Craig and Mark were both led over to the bench and gagged. A length of rope was threaded through their handcuffs and pulled tight forcing them to bend forward. The other length of rope was used to secure their legs to the legs of the bench, making movement impossible. A leather strap was produced and while the girls looking on horrified, their jeans and underpants were pulled down and six strokes were applied to their bare buttocks. Neither boy had experienced pain like it before but struggle as they might they could not escape it. They wanted to scream loudly but the gag stopped all but the most muffled of sounds. When they were released they were taken into the small office and made to stand facing the wall.

The girls were led over to the bench and the woman with the large breasts gave them three strokes each with the strap, and although they were allowed to keep their underwear on it was still no less painful. Five minutes later they were blindfolded again and put in the back of the van where they lay on the floor.

They heard the shutters going up and the noise of the engine as the van pulled out. A short while later they stopped at an old disused gravel pit. The officer in the back removed the blindfolds and the handcuffs and opened the door. He told them to wait there until help arrived. Craig and Mark had no intention of going anywhere. The pain was still bad enough to make walking hard work.

"Why did you have to tell them we did it?" wailed Amanda. "We'll have a criminal record now that we signed that paper."

Wendy stared at her. "They weren't the police, stupid. *They* wouldn't take us to an empty building and beat us."

"Course they were the police," snarled Craig, "and we can sue them for what they did to us, bloody perverts."

"Grow up, Craig," snapped Wendy. "They were them vigilantes that were in the paper, not the police." She too was still feeling the pain but not as bad as the boys. "They're not perverts either. We only got what we deserved."

"So what?" sneered Craig. "We don't have to say that to the real police when we report what they did."

"We're not saying anything."

"Oh yes we are!" chimed in Amanda and Mark together. "They're not getting away with what they did."

Wendy looked round at each of them, suddenly disgusted with what they had been doing and determined that from this moment on things were going to change. "If anyone says anything," Wendy hissed, "I'll tell the police everything that we done, including the shoplifting and the stone dropping."

"Then you'll get yourself in trouble," Amanda told her.

"I don't care," she snapped back. "But what will your parents say when they find out their precious daughter is a thief who drops stones on moving traffic. What will they think if they find out what you and Craig have been doing on his bed?"

Amanda held her hands to her mouth. "You wouldn't."

"I would. I'd tell them about everything and we'd all be put away. So keep your mouth shut." She paused and added, " I really don't want to find out what lesson two is, do you?"

Just then an ambulance arrived and they were ushered into the back and whisked off to hospital. The hospital informed the police that four children had been brought in having been severely beaten. The officer taking the call thought it might be the vigilantes again and contacted Inspector Burgess direct. Less than ten minutes later he and Jenny Tate were at the hospital.

They spoke to a doctor who told them, "It's a serious beating, probably with a leather belt. The boys are worse, but they'll get over it in a few days, physically anyway."

"Can we talk to them?"

"Oh yes," he said, "come with me." He led the way into a small room. When he saw who the children were he knew for sure that the vigilantes had been at work again.

"Well, well!" He turned to Jenny. "Have you met the Sharks, Constable?" He pointed to the boys. "This is Craig and Mark Thomas and this," he waved an arm at the girls, "is Amanda Green and Wendy Miles." The children looked at the floor and said nothing. "All right, what happened to you?"

"We got slapped," said Wendy.

"Slapped! The doctor told me you were beaten with a leather belt. Who did it?" There was silence. Colin looked at Jenny Tate and then back at the children. "Well! Is someone going to tell me what happened?"

"We got slapped," Wendy repeated. Mark opened his mouth to say something but she stopped him by glaring at him hard and adding, "We're saying nothing else." And no matter how hard

Colin and Jenny tried, they could not get another word out of them.

Cliff Miles, Wendy's stepfather, turned into Bradley Street and stopped his battered Sierra outside Number 6. He would normally have been at work this time of the day, but a phone call from Shirley telling him to come home as Wendy had been taken to hospital had been enough excuse for him to take the rest of the day off. He didn't know what was wrong with Wendy but he hoped it was nothing serious as he was almost on the verge of giving her some practical sex lessons.

He pushed open the driver's door but before he could get out, Shirley appeared. "Stay there," she told him, "we're going to the hospital." Shirley was twenty-eight and was dressed in a tight black skirt with a white blouse, neither of which did anything to hide the curves of her body. The white high-heeled shoes accentuated the length of her very attractive legs that were clad in nylon stockings. Gold dangling ear rings swung from side to side under her shoulder-length peroxide-blonde hair. Bright red lipstick, thickly applied, completed the picture. Shirley thought she looked like a lady. Cliff thought she looked very sexy, and everyone else, including Wendy, thought she looked like a tart. Although she was concerned about her daughter, she had been none too pleased when a policeman called to tell her the news and she had to cancel her afternoon bingo session.

Arriving at the hospital they were told briefly, by a very young and very weary looking doctor, where the children were. He added that, although it was not his case, he was sure there was no serious injury and advised them that they could probably take Wendy home with them. Cliff was happy about that and started to think of excuses that would enable him to stay home and look after her, especially if she were to stay in bed.

Colin Burgess had seen them arrive – they were both well known to him. He nudged Jenny and indicated that she should follow him. They stopped the couple in the corridor and told them what had happened to their daughter.

"My Wendy, beaten with a belt!" she exclaimed in a high-pitched grating tone. "What bastard would do a thing like that?"

"We don't know for sure, Mrs Miles. None of them will say anything."

"What do you mean none of them?" interrupted her husband. "How many were there?"

"Her three friends were with her."

"What!" screamed Shirley. "Them Thomas boys and that stuck up little cow Amanda. Is that who you mean?" Colin looked at her but said nothing.

It was Jenny who said, "All we want is for you to have a word and see if you can get Wendy to tell you what happened. If none of them says anything we won't be able to do anything." Shirley put a cigarette in her mouth, but was reminded by a passing nurse that smoking was only allowed outside. She removed the cigarette, put it back in the packet and then stuck two fingers up to the nurse's back, muttering, "Bossy cow." Turning to the policeman, she said, "If Wendy won't tell you anything she's hardly likely to tell me, is she, and I can't force her, can I?"

With that she flounced down the corridor and into the room where Wendy was, closely followed by Cliff. The Inspector stared after her watching the cheeks of her bottom struggle in the confines of her skirt.

At eleven o'clock that evening as Cliff Miles walked back

alone from the pub, he was approached by two men. One produced a warrant card and in a broad Scottish accent said, "A word in your ear, Mr Miles." Cliff stopped walking and stared at the face. He noticed the scar that ran the length of one cheek.

"Yeah, whaddya want?" he asked.

"Just want to give you a bit of advice."

Cliff looked puzzled. "Advice?" he queried.

"Aye. Tomorrow, pack your case, climb into your Sierra and leave Temsley. Don't tell anyone you're going and don't under any circumstances come back."

Cliff was outraged. "You can't order me to do that," he spluttered. "Who do you think you are?" He lowered his face and glared at this strange copper. "You can fuck off, mate, I'm not going anywhere and you can't make me."

The second man who, up to that point, had said nothing, moved behind him. Cliff turned his head but the Scottish accent continued, "If you don't go, Mr Miles, two things will happen. Both your legs will be broken and you will be arrested and charged with sexual offences against a minor which will label you a paedophile."

The colour drained from his face and he started to panic inside. "What the fuck has Wendy told you?" he blustered. "I haven't touched her and you can't prove it."

"Why do you think I meant Wendy, Mr Miles?" The second man suddenly grabbed Cliff's arms and held them tight behind his back. "First thing in the morning," droned the Scot, "leave, and don't go near Wendy. Remember your legs, paedophile." With that he lifted his foot and gave Cliff a vicious kick in the testicles. He made a grunting sound and went down like a sack of potatoes. "There are no second chances, Mr Miles."

CHAPTER 11

The hall clock struck seven as Andy Mills let himself into his bachelor flat after a long, hot, tiring day. He picked up the letters that were spread on the floor and dumped them on the side-table. Going into the kitchen he opened the freezer, took out a ready-prepared meal, set the timer on the microwave and switched it on. While it hummed away and his dinner spun round and round, he removed his jacket, hung it on a peg in the hall, picked up his mail and went back into the kitchen.

The only thing of interest was a package similar to the one he had received after the Bannerman incident. He studied the outside, but all that told him was that it was posted in Temsley and sent first-class. Tearing open the flap he removed the contents: a video and two printed sheets. He began to read. The first paragraph was a warning. All the children whose names and addresses were listed below were under age, therefore their identities had to be kept secret. It went on to say they had owned up to being responsible for the Mile End Road crash, and all had signed a statement to that effect. He went to the VCR, pushed the cassette in and switched on. It was an eye-opener, and although he thought it no more than they deserved, he felt some sympathy for them. He phoned his editor, Barney Marshall, at his home.

"I've just received another package from the vigilantes," he said excitedly. "This time it's children and there's a video of what happened."

"Children!" Barney exclaimed. "You mean it shows children's hands being ..."

Andy interrupted him. "No, no, nothing like that – just four children being beaten."

"Beaten!" came the shocked reply. "My God."

Andy started to get a little frustrated. "No, not that either. More of a good old-fashioned spanking only a bit harsher. It's better if you see the video. I can be with you in ten minutes."

"Right." The line went dead.

Andy pulled at his right ear and thought, 'Seems like someone is doing something about the crimewave at last. I wonder who?' He heard the ping of the microwave as it informed him his dinner was ready. He removed it, placed it on the side, decided he wasn't hungry anymore, grabbed his jacket from the peg and left to see Barney Marshall.

Half an hour later, having read the statement and watched the video, Barney said, "Bit harsh, don't you think?"

"So is dropping bricks on traffic," commented Andy. "Ask the drivers of those cars involved."

"At any rate, there's certainly no doubt about it now," Barney stated. "We have a gang of vigilantes on our doorstep."

"Yes, but – "

"But what?"

"But I don't think we should take the side of the victims – if you can call Bannerman and those four delinquent children 'victims'. I think the public in general will applaud what has happened. It might be harsh but it's more than anyone else has done and you never know, it might just work."

Barney Marshall looked unconvinced. "We can't condone this sort of behaviour, Andy, even if we thought it was right."

"You don't have to condone it, Barney, just report it. We'll publish the story tomorrow along with the results of the survey."

"Survey, what survey?"

"The survey I'm going to do on the streets of Temsley first thing in the morning. The nationals will be onto this, the television lot as well. This is a big story, Barney, and it's on our patch." He stood up. "I suppose I'd better inform Inspector Burgess that I've received another package."

As he made his way back home he wondered why the vigilantes had picked him to send this information to. Why not the nationals? Papers like The Sun would undoubtedly come down on their side, they were always running stories about how stupid the law was. This sort of thing would be right up their street. He wondered if he might know the perpetrators as they surely had to be locals.

Colin Burgess knew, or rather he had assumed, that Andy would have received information about the Sharks, so he was not surprised when he phoned to tell him.

"Don't go printing any names, Andy," he warned. "Just remember the information is only hearsay. There is no evidence to suggest that the children had anything to with the stone dropping. The statement they have supposedly signed is not in the information I have received. Nor yours either, I suspect."

"Come on, Colin," Andy tried to sound hurt. "Not all the press is irresponsible, you know. I am just informing you that I have received another package. It does prove one thing, though."

"Oh, and what's that?"

"We definitely have a gang of vigilantes operating in Temsley, and Groucho is not going to like that one bit, especially when he sees the headlines tonight."

The policeman groaned inwardly. "Thanks a lot, Andy." He sighed. "Just don't mention vigilantes and police sources in the same article. I don't want Groucho to think that anyone here thinks along those lines, not out loud, anyway."

"Marks seems to be more than a bit paranoid about vigilantes," suggested the reporter. "I wonder if he's got anything to hide."

"Bloody hell, Andy, don't start imagining things about him. If you cast even the smallest shadow over him he'll come down on you like a ton of bricks. Me too, I shouldn't wonder."

"Don't worry, Colin, I wouldn't do anything like that." He sniggered, "The editor wouldn't let me. Still, it makes you wonder, doesn't it?"

"No, it doesn't. Goodbye." Colin put the phone down and stared at it as though expecting it to ring again. 'Groucho with something to hide,' he thought, 'that's a laugh. Still, he could have a mistress somewhere.' That thought made him laugh out loud. 'No, not even that, he's too much of a moaning old sod to have a mistress.'

The survey that Andy Mills conducted on the streets of Temsley could not, by any stretch of the imagination, have been classed as fair or even representative, although he spoke to about a hundred people. He picked those he spoke to very carefully – housewives, manual workers, estate agents, and an insurance broker or two. The questions were also very carefully worded so that he could get the answers he wanted, and at the end of it all, he was able to say quite truthfully that four out of five, or eighty percent, approved of the vigilante action even if the methods were considered harsh. He faxed through the results of the survey to the local television station and that afternoon Groucho found himself the centre of attention in front of the cameras. He seemed to enjoy the experience but baulked at the mention of vigilantes.

That evening, after he had read the local paper and complained to his wife about the 'rubbish' they printed, he sat down to watch himself on the local news. The interview he had given had been edited to such an extent that they had him saying things he had not said. The overall impression was that he knew it was the work of vigilantes and that, not only did he not condemn it, but actually pointed out that legislation such as the Police & Criminal Evidence Act had made the job of the police even more difficult. He was left fuming and immediately contacted the television station to complain. However, the damage was already done and he would have the unpleasant job of explaining the interview to the Chief Constable.

When Jack arrived at the police station the following morning, the main topic of conversation was the incident concerning the Sharks, or rather what had happened to them. In the locker room Jack listened as the police officers filled him in on the details. He managed to look suitably surprised and even show some signs of shock.

One officer that Jack knew only as Tom said, "Serves the little bastards right. I bet they don't do anything like that again."

"Come on, Tom," argued Jack, "surely the parents must take some of the blame for the actions of their offspring? They probably never had the chances you had."

"Bollocks," Tom replied. "You can't blame the Minister of Transport when someone gets drunk and has an accident in their car. Those little toe rags – and they are all known to us, especially the Thomas brothers – the only thing they never had is proper punishment. But they got that yesterday. Mind you, having said that, although I don't condone the actions of vigilantes, those toe rags don't deserve your sympathy either."

Jack was rather surprised at the outburst. "Still a bit brutal, though, beaten with a leather strap."

Tom had reached the door but he turned round. "I'm

surprised at you, Jack. Being a military man, I thought you would have agreed with tough discipline." He smiled, "Mind you, you've always been a soft bugger."

Jack turned to the others who had been listening, pointed both hands at his chest and exclaimed, "Me, soft? Do you lot think I'm soft?"

"As grease," said one.

"Warm butter," said the other. They both laughed and made their way up the stairs to their parade room. Jack was secretly pleased at what they had said about him being soft and was glad he'd kept his real opinions to himself. If everyone thought he was like that, it suited him down to the ground.

The punishment meted out to Bannerman and the Sharks had each been a trial run to see how the operation would go. The equipment needed to pass as police officers had been ridiculously easy to come by, and Lucy's skills at makeup made sure that none would be recognised. Although he was certain that getting information would not be a problem, Jack was surprised at just how straightforward it was. He was able to access the files and print them off, including photos of some of the most prolific shoplifters, car thieves, and general vandals, many of whom were still at school, as easy as if he were picking up the pages from a desk. As he had guessed, the passwords used by policemen were unbelievable. He knew that they had to be changed every forty days, but even so he couldn't foresee problems. When they changed the second time he would just revert to the earlier passwords. He knew that, like him, the police would alternate between two passwords because it was the easiest thing to do.

After the Sharks episode there was a lull in their activities. It was thought safer to do nothing during the summer while the children were not at school. There were too many risks. They just bided their time and collected the information they needed for when they started up again in September. The press would have more or less forgotten them by then and although they were unhappy about that, they knew they would make up for it. Oh yes, they would certainly make up for it.

Andy Mills was disappointed that the vigilantes had stopped. He was hoping to make a comparison with the crime figures on a 'before and after vigilante' basis. He was certain that there would be a dramatic effect. He was at a loss to understand why they had stopped. Colin Burgess, on the other hand was grateful.

CHAPTER 12

One evening in early September when the weather was cooler and the nights were drawing in, Martin Lloyd was arrested by the police. At the age of fifteen he was Temsley's most notorious car thief although he, like the press, called himself a 'joy rider'. Everyone, including Martin, had forgotten all about the vigilantes that had been active in early July. He hadn't stolen a car for more than a week so he wasn't too worried about being picked up. It was only when he was pushed into the back of a police van, handcuffed and blindfolded, that he started to worry. And it was not until he found himself in an empty building instead of a police station, that he remembered the vigilantes and started to panic.

After some persuasion he admitted being a car thief and signed a statement to that effect. He made a list of the cars he remembered stealing. It went into double figures. He never forgot the make and colour of the cars and sometimes he even remembered the registration numbers. Occasionally he knew the owners. The cars were always burnt out. As he was led over to the work bench someone started to hum a tune. The humming continued while he was beaten on bare buttocks with a leather strap. The beating stopped when blisters formed and he started to bleed. He was then taken south of the river, tied to a tree, gagged and warned that he either stopped his criminal behaviour or he would be taught Lesson 2.

"Just remember what happened to Bannerman," the Scottish voice whispered. He was then told that an ambulance and the police would be with him shortly. A card was hung round his neck declaring:

I AM A CAR THIEF AND THIS IS LESSON 1

A brother-and-sister team of shoplifters, David and Lisa Jackson, received the same treatment. In their statement they indicated where the stolen property was kept until it was sold. After the police had picked them up they acted on the information that was left at the scene with them. They discovered a veritable treasure trove of stolen property, most of which still had the shop price tags on. The Jacksons too were warned about Lesson 2 and reminded of Bannerman. The card round their necks told everyone:

WE ARE THIEVES AND STEAL FROM SHOPS

A graffiti artist was caught in the act of spraying a bus stop shelter. He had also sprayed road signs and a telephone box that had been cleaned of his artistry just that day. He too made a statement admitting the offences and to stealing cans of spray paint from the local cycle shop. He too was beaten and warned what would happen if he did not stop. He was stripped to his underpants and sprayed on the back, chest and legs with the paints he had with him, and, under cover of darkness was tied to the slide in the children's playground opposite Riverside Apartments where Bannerman lived, with a card round his neck stating:

I AM THE PERSON WHO SPRAYS GRAFFITI EVERYWHERE.
THIS IS LESSON 1

In three weeks, nine juveniles received the vigilante treatment. Each time, Andy Mills received the information that the police had and his paper was full of it. The local television news ran the story practically every day, and by the beginning of October there wasn't one person in Temsley who hadn't heard of the vigilantes. Not that the public were yet fully aware of it, but the effect the vigilantes were having on the crime rate was quite dramatic. Shoplifting decreased, graffiti became almost non-existent, and car theft, along with minor criminal damage became something of a rarity. Schools noticed a marked improvement in attendance and behaviour patterns, although neither the police nor the schools released that information.

Opinions on the activities of the vigilantes were divided. The police naturally condemned it as criminal behaviour, and ironically and probably for the first time ever, the villains of Temsley agreed with them. Privately, some of the police were overjoyed that at last something positive was being done to deter crime. Many of the law-abiding citizens of the town were in complete agreement with what they were doing and publicly applauded their actions. There were many cries of 'bring back the birch' and 'restore corporal punishment in schools', but the government of the day did what they always did in such circumstances – they ignored it.

The arguments went back and forth. A few residents of the town screamed about civil liberties and the human rights of those being so harshly punished, but the vast majority responded by asking 'What about the rights of the victims who have suffered because of these criminals?' And so it went on.

Inspector Burgess was at a loss. There were no real clues. The victims had all given statements to the police, albeit reluctantly, but they either didn't know much, or just weren't saying. The public were equally silent too, although that did not surprise him one bit. It was only what he had expected. The vigilantes were not only very clever but very well informed. They did their homework thoroughly. Colin Burgess was sure, nonetheless, that sooner or later they would make a mistake and get caught. The trouble was, if that happened, the crime rate would revert to how it was before they came on the scene. While secretly applauding what they were doing, Colin was bothered by the possibility that they might eventually start dishing out more permanent and fatal punishment, thus setting themselves up as executioners.

The one thing that the majority did not agree with was that some of those who had initially admitted to the offences were not prosecuted because they later denied it. The official reason was that a conviction, if there was one, would be deemed unsafe because the confessions were made under duress.

At three o'clock on October 6th, Andy Mills drove round to Riverside Lane, parked the car and looked at the blocks of flats known as Riverside Apartments. He found the block that housed number 29 but discovered that he needed to contact the resident before being allowed inside. He knew that Bannerman wouldn't talk to him if he buzzed up and said he was from the press, but he couldn't think how else to get in. Seeing someone coming towards the door from the inside he pretended to speak into the microphone on the wall. The resident coming out opened the door just as Andy said, "Right, John." Then he looked up and added "Good afternoon."

The resident nodded and without a second glance held the door open for him. He padded up the stairs to number 29 and knocked on the door. He had been surprised when the magistrates had allowed Bannerman bail, but it gave him a chance to try and talk to him. There was a spy hole in the door and he could tell he was being observed. The door opened slightly, held on a chain.

"Yes? Who are you and what do you want?"

Andy held up his identification card. "I would like to ask you a few questions, Mr Bannerman."

"Christ Almighty, don't you coppers ever give up?" The door closed, the chain rattled loose and the door opened a little wider. "You'd better come in, I suppose."

Andy could hardly believe his luck. Being taken for a policeman was something he hadn't bargained on and he decided to make the most of it.

"I've told you blokes all I know about the assault on me," Bannerman continued, "and if you want to talk about anything else I want my solicitor present."

Andy stood by the large picture window and looked round. The flat was quite large. He'd come down a passage to get to this room, the lounge, and he had noticed four other doors leading, he supposed, to bedrooms, bathroom, and kitchen. The window he stood at overlooked the river and he gazed in the direction of Southbridge Road. A number of swans had gathered at the water's edge as people stopped to throw them titbits. Turning back to the room and the thin figure of Bannerman, he noticed that his hands were still bandaged up although he had use of the thumbs. He looked very drawn and there were bags under his eyes as though sleep was difficult.

"All I want, Mr Bannerman, is for you to tell me what happened that night. New information has come to light and – "

Bannerman interrupted him. "How many more times do you want telling? I've told the story to at least three of you lot." He held his hands up. "This is what fucking happened."

"I know that, but tell it to me. You might just remember something that could tie in with this new information."

He sighed and began to relate the story once more. Andy listened but there didn't seem to be anything that would help.

Bannerman ended by saying bitterly, "The bloke that did this," he held up his hands, "was mad. He even hummed a tune as he did it."

"Really? What was the tune, Mr Bannerman?"

"Like I said before, I don't bloody know, it was just some poncey tune." Suddenly his face showed signs of recognition and he added triumphantly, "Yes I do know, it was that tune from the film Wilmer Madrigal."

Andy looked puzzled for a moment. "Do you mean Elvira Madigan?"

"Yeah, that's the one. I took a girl to see it."

Andy stood up. "Well, I think that's all. Thank you for your time, Mr Bannerman."

He left the flats wondering how on earth the information he had would help. The theme tune from Elvira Madigan was a Mozart piano concerto, or rather the second movement of one, and it seemed a funny thing to hum while you smashed someone's hands with a hammer. He remembered someone else humming that tune recently, but he couldn't think who it was. Try as he might he just could not remember. Leaving Riverside Lane, he turned left into East Street and right into Bradley Street where the Sharks lived. He wondered if any of the children had heard someone humming a tune when they were being beaten. The only way to find out was to ask them.

As he turned into the street the now defunct Sharks were on their way home from school. Craig and Mark Thomas had surprised everyone when they had turned up at school and asked if they could come back. The headmaster had at first refused, but when they started to plead and promise to behave themselves in the future, he gave them one final chance. True to their word, they did behave themselves and their aggression had all but disappeared. In addition, it was discovered that they were both quite bright academically and although they had a lot of catching up to do, it seemed they were up to it. Since the beating and the threat from Wendy about spilling the beans on all their past activities, they had changed beyond all recognition.

Amanda and Wendy too had started to go to school regularly again and had become firm friends. Wendy's home life had improved dramatically since her stepfather had left. The anxiety she had felt every time she stepped into the house had been lifted. Her mother never knew why or where he had gone. He had just packed his case the morning after the Sharks had been beaten and drove off in his battered Sierra. Shirley had pleaded with him to stay but he took no notice. She stood on the doorstep screaming abuse and accusing him of having another woman as the car roared up the road and disappeared.

Wendy, though, was convinced it was the vigilantes' doing and not another woman. She remembered the way the man had looked at her when he said 'No we're nothing like your stepfather' and had made a note of something. No, his disappearance was nothing to do with another woman, but she didn't tell her mother that. Other things were different too. She found that she quite enjoyed school. The teachers had changed and the new ones had introduced her to computers, something she found she had a particular interest in.

Amanda had been glad that she and Craig hadn't 'done it'. The threat from Wendy about telling her parents had somehow made her see sense. She also perceived Craig for what he really was, a bully and a troublemaker. She could see he wasn't like that anymore, but both she and Wendy had agreed it was best to avoid the Thomas brothers since *that* day. At school she had discovered a flair for design and had decided that, when she left, she would like to be a clothes designer. She and Wendy chatted as they turned into Bradley Street.

"Who's he?" Amanda asked pointing to the stubby man emerging from the garden of number 6. Wendy looked over and took in the brown suit and shoes. She seemed to recognise him as he looked over his glasses in their direction.

"I'm not sure," she replied, "but I seem to know him from somewhere."

"Not your mum's new boyfriend, is he?"

Wendy smiled. "I shouldn't think so. Anyway, she's gone off men."

The stranger waited at the gate as they approached. "Hello, Wendy, Amanda, remember me?"

"No," said Wendy, "who are you?"

"I'm the reporter who was sent the information about what happened to you." Wendy pushed past him and shut the gate. "I only want to ask you if any of the people were humming a tune when they … er … beat you."

She turned and walked down the short path, put the key in the door and called out, "See you later, Mandy. Don't say anything to him." She opened the door and was gone.

"Right," said Mandy and started to walk to her own house.

"Well?" Andy urged, walking after her.

"Well what?"

"Are you going to do what she says or are you going to tell me if anyone was humming."

"Whistling," she said, "one of them was whistling."

"Ah! What was the tune, do you know?"

"No, I don't. Why do you want to know?"

The brown-suited man shrugged his shoulders. "I'm trying

to find out what sort of person would do – what they did to you."

She stared at him for a moment. "I don't know what it's called, but they play it when the show-jumping is on the telly." She turned and walked on.

He watched as she walked up the garden path and disappeared into her house, then decided it was time to leave that grotty street.

CHAPTER 13

Jack made his way up the stairs to his office and switched on the computer. Checking the phone for messages, he was relieved to discover there were none. He went into the room where the traffic wardens gathered. On seeing him they began to pick up notebooks, radios, and hats.

"Any problems?" he asked. There was a shaking of heads. "Right, well, let's get on then, shall we?" One by one they left the office to walk the streets and terrorise stationary motorists.

Opposite Jack's office was the Police Federation room. It was for the most part unused – the main bulk of their work was done at another office in the Force HQ building. It was, however, fully equipped, including a computer linked in to the police main-frame. It was where Jack went when he wanted information and it was to this room that he headed now. Having made sure there was no one around, he went in and closed the door.

He switched the computer on and waited while it buzzed into life. The urge to light up a cigarette was almost overpowering but he managed to resist the temptation by forcing himself to concentrate on the task in hand. Using the password that he had seen Pete Allen, a CID sergeant use, he found himself in at level 1. Selecting level 2 he typed in LINDA, the name of Pete's wife, at the password prompt. An error message appeared so he typed in ROVER, the name of Pete's dog. The screen changed and he was in. Selecting CRIME FILE, the screen changed again, prompting him for yet another password. He typed in 1234, which was the default password, knowing that

Pete would be too lazy to change it even though he should.

When the screen changed again, he selected DRUGS, and typed in TEMSLEY. A list of eight names appeared. Selecting them one by one to find the extent of their activities, he finally settled on BAKER. He pushed the print button and waited as the printer produced three sheets of paper containing all the information there was on him. Shutting the computer down, he picked up the printed sheets and went back to his office. The whole process had taken less than ten minutes. No one had seen him enter or leave the Federation room. Putting the sheets in his brief case he turned to his computer, accessed the e-mail facility and began his own work for the day.

When he arrived home that evening he found Lucy by herself. "Charlie has decided to move out," she told him. "He's found a little flat and has decided to stay there until his house is sold and he can move into more permanent accommodation."

"I really didn't think he would sell the house, not once he'd got over the initial shock."

"You saw the house before it was all smashed up, didn't you?" Jack shook his head.

"No," he said sadly, "I hadn't been there since the day of the funeral, except the day *after* it was wrecked, and there was no way of telling what it used to be like."

"The whole place was a shrine to Sue and Karen. Everything was just as Sue had left it. The lounge, dining room, Karen's room, even their bedroom. He never slept in it. It was as though he were waiting for them both to come home." She put her hands on Jack's shoulders. The closeness was electrifying and he wanted to reach out to her, to kiss her, to touch her, but he did none of those things. "Those two men wrecked his life along with his house, and all for a handful of jewellery." She sighed and shook her head. "I don't think he'll ever get over the loss of all those personal items." Jack nodded understandingly then bent down to retrieve his briefcase, breaking the contact of her hands on his shoulders. He withdrew the printed sheets and placed them on the table.

"Charlie will be interested in these," he said as he sat down, Lucy behind him, renewing the contact. His senses started to reel as the aroma of her perfume drifted into his nostrils. Fighting to control the urge to take her in his arms he added, "This is about Nick Baker and it would seem almost certain that the two who wrecked the house would have got their drugs from him."

"Are you sure it wasn't that chap Bannerman who did the damage?"

"Positive, and so are the police, otherwise they would have charged him with that too. No, the only thing Bannerman would ever break is someone's bones."

"So, what about this Nick Baker?"

Her hands were caressing his shoulders and her thumbs began to massage the back of his neck. Talking was becoming difficult and it was hard to concentrate, but he managed to say, "He's a nasty little scumbag who deals in drugs, mainly supplying children from fourteen upwards. He's been caught but only for possession of a small amount, so all he got was community service. The intent to supply could never be proved. However, sources say that he's dealing and deflowering girls from the local schools while they're under the influence. Ecstasy tablets that were responsible for causing two deaths are known to have come from him, but there's no hard evidence."

"Meanwhile," commented Lucy, "he is still selling drugs and indulging in under-age sex."

Jack nodded. "That's about the size of it. There's also a warning on the sheet that he could be HIV positive, but that's not definite."

Lucy opened her eyes wide in horror, gasped, and stopped the massage. "Jesus! If he is, it means he's infecting those young girls. Are we going to stop him?"

Jack smiled. "Not tonight, Lucy. I'm hungry."

He stood up and looked in her eyes. He was about to take a chance and kiss her when she said, "It's a good job I prepared dinner, then, isn't it? Go and wash, it will be on the table in ten minutes." With that she went into the kitchen and left him wondering how soon he would get another chance.

The meal was eaten mostly in silence although the looks that each gave the other spoke volumes as to their thoughts. The meal over, they set to work clearing away the dishes and washing up. The work involved being in close contact and they both ensured that there was plenty of touching and brushing against one another without being too obvious. Job finished, they went back into the lounge.

"Are you going to phone Charlie?" she asked.

"Tomorrow," he replied.

Lucy moved closer, gazed into his eyes and put her hands back on his shoulders.

"Lucy," he whispered, "you know what I'm like. I'll only hurt you." She smiled up at him and he knew without a shadow of a doubt that he loved this woman, had always loved her.

"Of course I know what you're like, Jack Templeton, and I can assure you, you won't hurt me." She pulled him towards her and all resistance left as their lips touched. Picking her up in his arms he carried her up the stairs and all other thoughts disappeared like snowflakes on a hot plate.

It was the following afternoon when Lucy phoned her brother and told him what Jack had got on Nick Baker.

"Contact the others," he said. "Nick Baker is next on our list."

Their target lived in a small block of flats, owned by an absentee landlord, in Jackson Close on the Eastley Estate. It was a particularly seedy part of town and the flat wasn't much to write home about, but it suited him. He felt safe in these flats. No one was nosy and no one would talk about anything that went on, which was the reason he was so successful. Everyone in the flats had something to hide so no one co-operated with the police, or anyone else.

He looked at the naked girl on the bed and wished he could spare another half an hour. The girl, Emma Jennings, was only fifteen and, as he had discovered, had been a virgin. It was worth giving the lads freebies now and again, he thought, especially when they managed to get girls like Emma to come round and try his wares. She had been nervous about taking the tablet at first, but when he told her that the effects lasted less than two hours she had succumbed. In less than ten minutes he was undressing her without any objections at all, in fact she giggled. She had not objected either when he pushed into her and had taken her virginity. He had managed it three times and still wanted more.

As he dressed she began to stir. She was still dreamy eyed and looked at him with a smile on her face.

"Hurry up and get dressed," he snarled, "I've got things to do."

She looked puzzled, and stared at him. "Get dressed?" It was then that she realised she was naked. She sat upright and drew her knees up to her chin in an attempt to cover herself. "You can't do it to me," she cried, "I'm a virgin."

Baker just sneered. "*Were* a virgin," he corrected. "I've already done it, three times in fact. Now get dressed." Emma started to cry. She didn't want to have done it with him, but she knew she must have, and was ashamed. Baker grabbed her hair and pulled it, making her cry out.

Putting his face close to hers he warned, "Get your bloody clothes on and don't go mouthing off to anyone about what happened here either. You wanted the pill and you were willing. I just obliged you. Anyway, if you want to keep those looks, keep this shut." He pinched her lips between his thumb and forefinger.

Emma climbed off the bed and started to put her clothes back on, conscious of his eye on her every move. Her clothes were her school uniform, and as Baker watched he thought how much of a turn-on that had been. He decided he would try something different with her if she ever came round again. She turned her back on him and bent to retrieve her knickers. He gave her a stinging slap on her bare bottom.

"Hurry up," he gloated, "or I might try for another three." She glared at him. "You bastard," she screamed, "what if I'm pregnant?" She hurriedly started pulling her clothes on.

"I use condoms, you silly cow. You ain't pregnant. Mind you," he sneered, "I wouldn't mind if that's what you want."

"Fuck off," she yelled.

He slapped her hard. The blow knocked her sideways and she sprawled on the bed. He pulled her up by the hair again and hissed, "Remember what I said about keeping your looks. If anyone comes round here because of you, you'll get it, even if I'm in the nick." He dragged her off the bed, and making sure she had picked everything up, pushed her out of the door and slammed it shut.

She shouted through the letter box, "You bastard!"

As Emma left the block of flats she saw a police van pull up in the small car park. She was in two minds about going over and telling them what had happened, but the thought of going to court, her parents finding out she had taken drugs and everyone knowing that he'd 'done it to her', was too much to bear, so she walked past. She reached the roadway and looked back. Three policemen were going in the block where Baker lived.

There was a knock on the door and Baker was angry. 'If it's that bloody girl,' he thought, I'll teach her a fucking lesson'. He opened the door slowly but it suddenly flew back in his face catching him down the side of his head from the eyebrow to the chin. He staggered back groaning as three police officers pushed their way into the flat. One forced him to the floor and put a knee on his chest.

"We want all the drugs in your flat, the money, and the name of your supplier." The voice had a soft Scottish burr. The knee moved and the officer stood up.

Nick's initial shock at the situation subsided, his cockiness returned and he gave a typical Baker reply. "You can fuck off." He usually said things like that to the police. Two officers were searching cupboards and he added, "You bastards better have a search warrant." He went to stand up but a boot crashed into his side sending him sprawling once more.

"Wrong answer," purred the Scottish voice. Baker lay on the floor clutching his side and moaning in pain. "We haven't got all day," snapped the voice. "Drugs, money, and supplier." It was a question Baker did not want to answer.

One of the officers who was searching called out, "If he won't answer, cut his throat. At least that will take him out of circulation."

The officer with the Scottish voice knelt down again. This time he was holding a large, ugly-looking knife. As the blade turned, the light glinted on it like an evil eye. It moved under his chin and Nick suddenly found his voice. "Wait," he screamed, "wait, I'll tell you." He told them where the drugs were hidden – in a fake baked bean tin and a half-open packet of cereals. His money was stashed in a small wall safe that looked like two electrical plugs set in the wall at the level of the skirting board. There was also a notebook full of names, and written next to a lot of them was the word 'school'.

"Is there any more?" asked the knife wielder. Baker shook his head. "You're a lying little bastard," hissed the voice. The knife moved down to his groin. "I hear you like sex." Baker felt the knife between his legs as the voice continued, "You won't be able to perform if I cut your balls off. Now, last time, is there any more?"

Baker was terrified. His stomach was churning and he was sweating profusely. Pointing to an armchair he croaked, "Under the floorboards, move the armchair." The pressure of the knife eased. The armchair was moved and the hiding place, very cunningly concealed by the pattern of the carpet, was discovered. The space underneath was full of freezer bags containing heroin, cannabis, and assorted pills. There was also a bag containing jewellery. Jack held it up. Charlie saw the bag and snatched it from him. There was anger on his face and he nodded his head toward the small kitchen. The questions stopped as Jack and Charlie disappeared into the small room.

"He's the bastard who supplied those fucking little toe rags that smashed up my place," Charlie hissed.

"You can't be sure of that," countered Jack.

"Oh yes I can." He held up the bag. "This jewellery you

found was Sue's. They must have come round here with it and he gave the bastards drugs in exchange."

The anger on his face was like nothing Jack had ever seen before and he had to do some quick thinking before it got the better of his friend.

"Calm down, Charlie, for Christ's sake. Anger will get us caught."

"I don't care if I'm caught, Jack, as long as he's out of circulation."

"What about the others, Charlie? Have some thought for them unless you want to see Lucy and the rest of us serving time."

The mention of Lucy in prison was like a bucket of cold water thrown over him. The effect was instantaneous and Jack could see the self-destructive anger draining from Charlie's face. He nodded and whispered, "I'm all right now, Jack, come on, let's get this over with." They went back into the other room and the questions began once again.

"Who supplies you?"

"Please," whined Baker, "if I tell you that he'll kill me."

The knife moved back to his throat and the point pierced his adams apple.

"If you don't, *I'll* kill you."

Nick Baker talked. "Jeff Spooner, he supplies me and others."

"Jeff Spooner?" The Scottish voice was loaded with disbelief.

"Yes. He's got a small transport firm on the Commercial Road Estate. He stores the stuff there. I swear it." The knife moved slightly and blood flowed from the small cut.

"Jeff Spooner, involved in drugs? You're a lying git." The knife moved away from his throat.

"No, I'm not," he babbled, "Curly Wilson helps him." He began to tell them all the information he had on Spooner. When he finished they pulled him to his feet.

"You're nicked, Baker. Give me your car keys." He handed them over and was led outside toward the waiting van.

The female officer, who had been waiting in the van, opened the rear doors and Baker was pushed inside. Two of the officers climbed in with him and pushed him to the floor. The third walked over to where his car, an old but serviceable BMW with an automatic gear box, was parked. Baker was still scared but felt relieved that he was actually in a police van. He had never known the police to act this way before. His ribs hurt like hell and he wondered if he could bring charges for assault against them but knew they would only say he had been resisting arrest. One of the officers leant forward and handcuffed his hands behind his back, then blindfolded him.

"What the fuck are you doing?"

Someone grabbed his hair and jerked his head up. "Keep your mouth shut," snarled a voice, and his head was slammed back down on the floor. The engine started and the van pulled away followed by Baker's car.

The area around the flats was deserted as the vehicles pulled into the road, except for Emma Jennings who stood, unnoticed, in the cover of some bushes. As the van passed her she whispered to herself. "Serves you right, you bastard, I hope you rot in hell."

Baker lay on the floor of the van unable to get up and too scared to say anything in case he got another kicking. He thought that the van was taking an extraordinarily long time to reach the police station, which at most was only ten minutes away, and wondered if they were going somewhere else. Just then he heard the crackle of a radio and the unmistakable chatter of police business. The van began to slow down and came to a halt. There was a clanking sound of metal shutters being raised. The van moved forward and the shutters clanked again as they rolled down. The doors of the van were opened, Baker was dragged out, and the blindfold removed.

He looked around and was shocked to discover that he was in an almost empty factory unit. Before he could say anything he was pushed towards a table. A tape recorder was switched on and he was asked a series of questions, many of which he had already been asked. It was pointless to keep quiet as they already had the information, the only difference was that now it would all be on tape. He was told to repeat the information about Spooner. The recorder was switched off.

"You ain't the police," Baker said accusingly. "I ain't seen any of you before." No one replied, simply stared at him. "If you was in the police," he added, "you must be on the make. How much do you want?"

Jack, who had been quietly humming the overture from the 'Marriage of Figaro', stepped forward and waved a fist in Baker's face. "We don't take kindly to being bribed. Anyway, we have everything you've got."

Baker stared at the fist and noticed the gold ring with the letter J engraved on it. He looked from the ring into Jack's face and then back at the ring. A look of recognition spread over his face. "I know you," he declared, "you're a traffic warden. You were in court with that other little git that tried to stitch up Dave Turner. I admired that ring then. Dead giveaway, that." He paused for breath with a smug look on his face.

Jack's face creased into a smile. "Clever little bastard, aren't you? Trouble is, you can't keep your mouth shut, can you?" The cloth that had been used as a blindfold was now used as a gag and he was bundled roughly into the back of the van again.

"What now, Jack," asked Ronnie quietly, "now that he knows who you are."

It was Charlie who answered. "The brick pit." They all stared at him. His face was a mask of hatred. Holding up the bag containing the jewellery they had found at Baker's flat he added, "This is Sue's. He's the bastard who supplied those addicts that wrecked my house. He deserves the brick pit." There was a stunned silence as he added, "The one past the Edgetown Estate is eighty foot deep at the edge. It'll be a long time before they find him, if they ever do."

"Kill him!" exclaimed Jack. "That's not a good idea."

"Why not? Two youngsters are dead because of him and if he is HIV positive how many young girls has he infected?" The others still just looked at him. "Anyway, it's not killing, it's just getting rid of some particularly nasty rubbish."

Jack shook his head. "I don't know, Charlie, I didn't think murder would be part of this."

"What then, Jack, let him go? He'll be round that nick with your name on his lips so quick his feet won't touch the ground and it wouldn't take a genius to fathom out who else was involved."

"He wouldn't do that, not with what we've got on him."

"What are you saying, Jack? Are you suggesting we do nothing with what we've got from him?"

"He's right, Jack," declared Ronnie, "we have to get rid of him."

Without another word the van was stripped of its police logo and blue light. That done, it was driven to the Edgetown brick pit along with Baker's BMW.

The pit in question was deserted, but just to make sure, two of them walked right round it. When they returned, they dragged Baker out of the van and pushed him into his car. He started to struggle but a solid punch on the jaw put a stop to that. He was tied to the steering wheel and all the windows were opened. The two polythene bags containing the drugs, cash, and notebook were stowed in the boot, which was then locked. The car was started up, a brick placed on the accelerator and the handbrake released. A broken branch was pushed through the passenger window and the gear lever was moved into 'drive.' The car shot forward, plunged over the ten-foot-high bank and into the water.

They watched silently as it started to sink, then waited five minutes just to make sure Baker did not somehow escape his fate. They ruffled the grass where the tyres had flattened it, put tree branches on the ground where it went in and then left. Their departure, like their arrival, went unnoticed. Only Nick Baker remained and he was in eighty feet of water.

CHAPTER 14

The Lion & Unicorn, where Charlie had arranged for them to meet, was a small hotel in Ely situated away from the town centre and surrounded by trees. It was close enough for everyone to get to easily, but far enough away so that there was minimal risk of being recognised or seen together. It was a comfortable place and Charlie had rented the room on behalf of the 'East Anglian Writers Circle'. The landlord, who also supplied food and drink when required, was always happy to make extra cash by renting a room out on an occasional basis, especially in early October, and he took the money gratefully. Up to then, Charlie and Jack had decided everything and passed on the information – Jack to Lucy and Ronnie, Charlie to Phil Ormisher. Now, with the death of Nick Baker, things were different and a group meeting was thought to be necessary.

Today they had to decide whether or not to carry on with what they were doing. Even though he hadn't been found yet and probably never would be, the stakes were different. They would now all face a murder charge if they were ever caught. No one had actually said that they wanted to stop, but the question was obviously there and had to be answered.

Charlie got straight down to business. "If anyone wants out, now's the time to say. There will be no arguments and no names will be mentioned if the rest are ever caught." He looked around the room expecting someone to speak, but there was silence. "Anyone?" Still silence. "The stakes are higher now that Baker is dead. It will be murder."

Ronnie Thompson spoke. "Look, Mr Slater, I think the silence is all the answer you need. No one here thinks Baker's death was anything but necessary. It's done and can't be undone. Anyway, if it was up to me, all the drug dealers and pushers would end up the same way."

Charlie smiled at the use of 'Mr Slater'. He turned to Jack. "What about you, Jack?"

Jack leaned forward in his chair and paused before answering. "I have to say that I'm not overjoyed about Baker's death, especially as I was the one he recognised, but as Ronnie says, it can't be undone. So I'm still with you, Charlie. The idea was to dish out some form of justice and hopefully to make some impression on the crime figures. I don't know if we have managed that yet."

Charlie looked at Lucy. She shrugged. "Count me in."

He turned to Phil. "What do you say, Phil?" The mechanic pursed his lips, screwed his eyes up, took a deep breath and said, "What are we going to do about Jeff Spooner?"

Charlie leaned back in his chair. The tension drained away and was replaced by a feeling of confidence.

"The first thing to do is make sure he really does deal in drugs," said Jack. "Even the police don't have any suspicions on that score and we can't take Baker's word, he was a born liar."

"So you think he was lying about Spooner?" Charlie said.

"I don't know," Jack replied. "Probably not, but let's say I wouldn't believe him if he swore blind he was telling a lie." The discussion went on for another two hours, then one by one they drifted off and made their way back to Temsley by different routes.

Baker's death was not reported to the police or the press and neither was the fact that his cash and drugs had been seized by the vigilantes. Most importantly, the information regarding Jeff Spooner was also kept secret. What was wanted now was proof of guilt and that was going to be a slow and difficult task. Keeping Spooner and Curly Wilson under surveillance was easier than they thought it would be, but finding evidence to prove his involvement was harder than they envisaged. Jack's opinion was that Spooner had the confidence of one who knows he was unlikely to be suspected of any crime, let alone drug dealing.

They soon discovered that during the day he never put a foot wrong. His associate, Curly Wilson, did have a record and had spent time in prison, but it was assumed by the authorities that Spooner's influence had changed him for the better. So Curly was watched and photographed every time he spoke to someone. Those people were then identified and Jack used his knowledge of the police computer system to get information on them. Some were known villains and others had no connection with crime of any sort, or at least there was nothing on record about them.

Spooner too was watched and photographed, but it was even more difficult to make any connection at all with drug dealing. He was a very well-known and generally respected man. He met the mayor, senior police officers including Superintendent 'Groucho' Marks, had dinner at various functions, gave money to charities and presented prizes at schools. He was known to favour certain projects including youth clubs and the rehabilitation of criminals back into society. All in all, he was cleaner than the proverbial whistle.

Something unusual then happened as Lucy was keeping watch on his factory unit. One of Spooner's vans turned up, and having reversed into the factory unit the shutters were closed down. This was very unusual and Lucy decided to try and find out what was going on. She climbed out of the car, crossed the road and walked into the office that was part of the warehouse unit. The office was empty, but through an internal window at the rear of the small room she could see the van at the far end. A fork-lift truck was lifting a pallet loaded with tyres. She saw Spooner with a case of some sort, duck under the pallet. There was a faint clang of metal and when he emerged the case was no longer with him. She watched as the tyre-laden pallet was lowered back into position, and turned to leave. At that moment a man in greasy overalls with the Spooner Transport logo over the right-hand breast pocket came through the outer door.

He smiled at her and asked, "Are you being attended to?" She wondered if he was anything to do with the drug side of the business and her brain went into overdrive.

"No. There doesn't seem to be anyone around." She hoped she didn't sound as panicky as she felt.

"Did you ring the bell?"

"Bell? Er, no." He strode over to where the bell push was situated on the wall and raised his finger.

"Maybe you could help me," she said quickly. He paused. "I only came in for some information about your rates."

He removed his finger. "Oh, that's no trouble at all," he said, as he moved over to the counter. He opened a drawer, pulled out some leaflets and handed her one. "These are the latest and I'm sure you'll find them very reasonable."

Lucy took the leaflet, thanked him for his help and left the office. She wanted to run up the road to her car and it took a lot of willpower not to hurry or look back. She drove straight back to the house, phoned Jack and arranged to meet him in town.

As they walked down the High Street, past the Mercury Shopping Centre, Lucy related what she had seen.

"It certainly seems very strange," said Jack thoughtfully, "but it could be innocent." He considered for a moment and added, "Contact Charlie and see what he thinks. Personally, I'm for going in." They parted company.

Three days after speaking to Amanda Green, Andy Mills discovered that the theme music he was searching for was a composition by Mozart called the Musical Joke. Apparently, Amanda had been right about show jumping as it was the theme used for the televised Horse of the Year show. He poured himself a glass of sherry, selected the piece, the Piano Concerto No. 21, and played the second movement. The beautiful melody filled his lounge as he sat in his favourite chair sipping his drink and letting the beauty of the sound wash over him. He wondered how many more of the vigilante's victims had heard someone humming or whistling Mozart melodies during their beating.

CHAPTER 15

When Jeff Spooner made his way home from a Rotary Club dinner it was almost midnight. He wondered about his driving ability but decided that he should be safe enough. He had had wine with his meal but only orange juice afterwards as he listened to the endless chatter, which he found both soothing and amusing. He had nodded vigorous agreement as the conversation turned to crime and drugs and suggested that the penalties were far too lenient. It had amused him to go along with them and wondered what these people would say if they knew about his own extra-mural activities.

Having said his farewells, he pulled out of the car park and drove home. Even though he was sure that he would not be over the limit he decided to drive extra carefully and keep well within the speed limits. Consequently he was surprised when he saw a flashing blue light in his rear-view mirror, and even more surprised when the headlights indicated that he should stop. He pulled over to the side of the road, wound down the window and waited as a police officer got out of the white police van and approached him.

"Good evening, officer." Spooner didn't recognise the officer and assumed he was a new man. "Is there a problem?"

"Would you switch off the engine and step out of the vehicle please, sir." Spooner frowned and thought, 'Surely he's not going to breathalyse me.'

He climbed out and stood by the roadside. The officer had a breathalysing kit in his hand. "I have a suspicion you have been drinking and therefore I am going to take a breath sample." He held up the tube. "I would like you to blow in here, sir – one long breath and don't stop till I tell you."

Spooner hesitated. "Look," he said, trying his best to sound authoritative and failing, "my name is Spooner." He paused to see if there would be any reaction but there was none. The officer just looked blankly at him. "Random breath tests are not legal yet, you know. I would have to have committed a motoring offence before you can do this."

"Is that so, sir? Well now, you were seen to be driving on the wrong side of the road as you came round the bend about a mile back. You crossed the double white lines and that is an offence." He handed him the tube. "One long blow if you please, sir." Spooner took hold of the tube. He didn't want to blow into it but knew he could be arrested if he refused. He thought about mentioning that he knew Superintendent Marks, but decided against that too. He took a deep breath and blew in the tube. The officer looked at the little box and then showed it to him. The light was red.

"There must be some mistake, officer. My name is Jeffrey Spooner and – " he was cut off mid-sentence.

"Well, Mr Spooner, there is no mistake. I am arresting you for driving whilst under the influence of alcohol. You do not have to say anything but it may harm your defence if you do not mention, when questioned, something which you later rely on in court." He felt the officer take his car keys, then he was handcuffed and led to the waiting van while the policeman slipped into the driving seat of his car. When he climbed into the back of the van he was astonished to see Curly Wilson sitting there with two other police officers.

"What an earth are *you* doing here?"

Curly shrugged his shoulders. "I'm not sure, Mr Spooner. They said something about having a class A substance with intent." Spooner went cold and he felt the colour drain from his face. His eyes narrowed and his heart began to pound, but he had to keep himself under control with those two officers present.

"What were you doing when they arrested you?"

Again Curly shrugged his shoulders. "I was just coming out of the pub. I'd had a couple of pints, that's all."

"Then what?"

"Then the van pulls up and they searched me. Then they arrested me for having a class A substance with intent to supply, put me in the van and asked where you was."

"What did you tell them?" Spooner hissed.

"Just that you were at that Rotary dinner thing. I didn't say nothing else, Mr Spooner, honest."

"Was there something else to say, then?" asked one of the officers. They both looked up at him but stayed silent.

Spooner sat back. It was uncomfortable with his hands behind his back, but he had to think. Did they suspect he was dealing in drugs? No, he was too careful for that. He tried to think if he had been followed or watched but he was certain he hadn't. He was equally certain Curly would not have had drugs on him or said anything, so they must have planted the drugs in order to justify a search. But who would give them information like that? Not Curly, that's for sure. Someone at the depot? No, he couldn't imagine anyone grassing. What about Baker? Yes, it must have been him. He hadn't seen him for a while. He must have been arrested and told them, the little bastard! He most probably got pulled in for shagging a twelve-year-old or something and did a deal. If he had, he'd kill the little shit.

The van slowed down, and looking up he was surprised to see they were outside his house.

"We want the keys to your warehouse, Mr Spooner." He was pulled from the van and marched down the front path.

"For God's sake," whispered Spooner, "what will the neighbours say? You'll ruin my reputation."

"If you're quiet they won't know, will they? The keys."

The officer who had been driving opened the front door and they went in. He nodded towards a closed door.

"They're in there, on the desk."

The keys were collected and they went back to the van. As they drove off he noticed that the officer who had driven his car stayed behind. He could see his world start to collapse around him knowing that if they searched the house, they would find the videos, and then, oh shit!

Phil Ormisher searched the house as thoroughly as he knew how. He was careful to wear gloves and made sure that he put everything back as neatly as he had found it. The house was a large expensive one in Richmond Way, one of a row of similar detached properties with large gardens and hedges ensuring they were not overlooked by their neighbours. As he had expected, he found nothing to connect Spooner with drugs or any other illegal activity.

In the lounge he noticed a cupboard about three-foot six inches high that ran the length of one wall underneath some bookshelves. It was locked. Phil hadn't come across any keys during his search which looked likely to open it, but he recalled an unfamiliar key on the ring with the car keys. He tried it and the cupboard clicked open. Inside, the shelves were lined with hundreds of videos. Wondering why anyone would lock up a cupboard full of videos, the titles gave him the answer. They were porn videos. He selected one called 'The Naughty Miss'. He plugged in the power cable, switched on the machine, inserted the tape and pressed PLAY.

It began with a young girl about eleven in a school uniform. She looked familiar but he was unable to place her. He watched the tape for a few more minutes then switched it off and removed it. He wanted to be sick and he wondered what sort of depraved person would enjoy watching that sort of filth. Spooner obviously did. He put the tape back in its box and took it with him out to the car. He drove down to Spooner's Transport Warehouse in Commercial Road where he knew the others would be waiting. On the way he suddenly remembered the little girl's name – Tracy Devlin.

When he arrived, he took Jack into the small office, told him what he had found and gave him the tape.

"Are you sure it's Tracy Devlin?" Jack asked.

"No doubt about it," came the reply, "you can see for yourself. But I warn you it's pretty disgusting stuff. I only saw about three minutes of it and I wanted to be sick."

Jack pondered the problem for a minute or two then said, "Say nothing for the moment. After we've got the drugs and the information about how it's brought into the country, we'll decide what to do with the filthy bastard."

Phil nodded and they went back into the warehouse where Spooner and Wilson had been tied up, blindfolded, and gagged. The gags were removed. The questioning was about to begin.

"What the fuck's going on?" shouted Spooner when the gag came off. "What are you playing at?"

A kick in the ribs made him groan with pain. "We're not playing, Mr Spooner," said a soft Scottish voice. "We want some answers to some very important questions. So, when we ask, you answer."

"Go to hell." He groaned in pain as the same boot kicked him in the ribs once more.

"Now, Mr Spooner, I have a tape recorder here. When I ask a question, you answer it. Ok?" The machine was switched on. "Now, then, we want all the drugs you have. Where are they?"

"Drugs! I haven't got any drugs!" The boot crashed into his ribs again. This time a bone was heard to crack. Spooner screamed and jerked backwards with the force of the blow.

"Where are they?" the voice insisted. "Believe me, this is nothing compared to what will happen if you don't tell me."

Spooner soon told them what they wanted to know. The fork lift was used to move the stacks of tyres and a manhole cover was exposed. Inside were four large metal containers, three of which contained drugs of various sorts but mostly heroin, and the fourth contained cash, a quarter of a million pounds.

"Now," said the Scottish voice pleasantly, "We want to know where you get the stuff and how you bring it into the country."

Spooner told them. Sitting on the floor of his own warehouse, tied up and blindfolded and in considerable pain, it was pointless not to now. He could hear someone whistling and recognised the tune as a Mozart rondo. He now knew for certain that these people were not police. They would never behave in this way. These must be the vigilantes that the papers had been full of recently. It was pretty clear that Baker had given the game away – he'd probably been threatened with death if he didn't speak. Maybe he was already dead. The thought made his blood run cold and he shivered involuntarily. If Baker was dead, he could be next. He suddenly realised he hadn't heard anyone ask

Curly any questions and he'd heard no sound from him at all. Maybe they had killed him first. Oh Jesus, he badly wanted to empty his bowels. Maybe this was a dream.

The whistling stopped and the Scottish voice drifted into his thoughts, dragging him back to reality. This was no dream.

"One more thing, Mr Spooner – Tracy Devlin. You know Tracy of course."

'Omigod,' he thought, 'they know.'

"Who else is involved?"

Spooner was silent. He was too scared to speak. Charlie, Lucy, and Ronnie, not having seen the videos, looked at Jack puzzled, but they said nothing.

"I won't ask you again, you disgusting pervert, I'll just castrate you with my nice sharp knife."

Spooner felt something moving in the area of his groin and he imagined the knife there. He felt the pressure on the knife increase and it was too much for him.

"No," he screamed, "please don't, I'll tell you everything you want to know."

"Who abducted Tracy?"

"Curly."

"On your orders?"

"Yes."

"How many more are in it with you?"

"Five." He started to cry.

"Names and addresses?"

Between sobs he managed to reel off the five names and addresses. He was asked to repeat the last one.

"Roy Marks," he whimpered. "Christ, if you were the police you would know he's Superintendent at Church Street station."

They all looked at one another with shock on their faces.

"How many other children have you abducted?"

"Four." He began to sob again.

Charlie bent down, reapplied the gag and indicated that they should all go into the office. When the door was shut, he asked, "What's going on Jack? What's this about Tracy Devlin?"

"Tell him, Phil." Phil told him what he had found at Spooners' house.

"Bloody hell," Charlie cursed, "now what do we do?"

Lucy spoke. "I think they should both join Nick Baker." Her face was expressionless and her voice as cold as ice.

"What about Marks and the others?" asked Jack. "If Spooner is dead we might not get the proof needed to convict them – and before you ask, I'm not in favour of killing them all."

Charlie made the decision. They made several copies of the audio tape, put all the drugs and money back into the manhole and replaced the tyres. Having done that, they bundled Spooner and Wilson into Spooner's car and Phil drove them back to Spooners' house. He parked the car in the garage and tied them both firmly in their seats. He put the video in the recorder, switched on the TV and left a note saying,

PLAY THE VIDEO THEN LOOK IN THE GARAGE

He unlocked the cabinet containing the other videos, left the doors wide open and walked out of the house, making sure the catch was up and the front door ajar. He made his way down to the shops at the bottom of the road and was picked up by the van, now minus its blue light and the police insignia.

A copy of the tape recording together with a letter of explanation was packed in a jiffy bag addressed to Andy Mills and pushed through the letter box of the local paper, along with two other packets. One was addressed to Inspector Burgess and the other to the Chief Constable. A phone call to Andy Mill's home informing him that a package awaited him at his office and suggesting he should go there right away, completed the arrangements. It was now three o'clock in the morning.

Having received the early morning phone call, Andy was now wide awake. He dressed hurriedly, went down to the offices of the Gazette and collected his packet. The letter asked him to contact Inspector Burgess at his home address at the phone number given and make sure he got the packet addressed to him. He was also to make sure he delivered the other packet to the Chief Constable. It also warned him against printing any of the information he'd been given until he got the go ahead, and against contacting any other police officer other than Inspector Burgess. It went on to say that the audio tape would explain the reasons why such precautions were necessary.

Andy picked up all three packages and set off for home. He settled himself in his armchair and switched on the tape. He could hardly believe what he was hearing and phoned Colin Burgess as soon as the tape was finished. The policeman was not too happy about being disturbed in what he considered was the middle of the night.

"Inspector Burgess," he grunted. His brain, like his body, was still half sleep.

"Colin, it's me, Andy Mills."

"Bloody hell, Andy, d'you know what time it is?"

"Yes I do, but this is red hot, Colin. The Mozart Men have been at it again. I have a package for you which you must have immediately."

"Who the bloody hell are the Mozart Men?"

"It's a name I've given to the vigilantes, but never mind that, you need to see this information now. Can I come over?"

There was a grunt from the other end of the line. "All right,

I suppose you'd better. But Andy, this had better be good or I might find some harassment charges that will stick on you." He gave him the address and put the phone down with more force than necessary.

At half past four in the morning Spooner and Wilson had been arrested on drugs charges and Inspector Burgess had contacted the Chief Constable at his home asking for an immediate interview with him. He gave him the package that Andy Mills had given him, then took three officers with him and arrested Superintendent Marks. Having deposited him safely in the cells, the same three officers were dispatched to arrest the four other people that Spooner had named in connection with the abduction of Tracy Devlin.

When a rather heavy-eyed Jack arrived for work at eight o'clock that morning, the station was alive with the news about 'Groucho' Marks and Jeff Spooner. He smiled to himself and for a change he began to hum Wagner's *Ride of the Valkyries*. Today was going to be a good day, a very good day indeed.

CHAPTER 16

The arrest of Superintendent Marks and Jeff Spooner exploded onto the scene in Temsley bringing with it television crews and newspaper reporters from all over the country. The town had seen nothing like it before. Many could not believe that respected citizens like Spooner and Marks were actually guilty of the crimes they were charged with, but in the case of Spooner at least, the evidence of the drugs was irrefutable. People began to feel they could trust no one, and inevitably, rumours started about other leading citizens.

The Gazette broke the story first having been given the go-ahead by Inspector Burgess.

THE MOZART MEN STRIKE AGAIN!

screamed the headline and went on to explain not only the stories about Marks and Spooner, but why the newspaper had called them by that name. From that moment on everyone referred to them as the Mozart Men, even the police.

Andy wondered if the police would refer back to some of the vigilante victims to find out if someone was humming or whistling as they were being thrashed. He concluded they most probably would. Lowering himself into his armchair he began to think things through. He was the centre of attention in both newspaper and television worlds, because he was the one chosen by the vigilantes as their first point of contact. However, despite the fact that he had wanted at least one more story in the nationals before he retired, he was not relishing the attention he was getting as much as he thought he would. He badly wanted to find out for himself who these people were, and in order to do that he needed time on his own. At the moment, though, wherever he went, the media in one form or another were not far behind him.

The fact that the vigilantes had chosen him made him wonder whether he knew them personally, or at least one of them. Mentally he went through a list of people he knew well, dismissing each name as it came up as just not having the opportunity, the intelligence, or the bottle. Heaving himself upright he glanced at the clock. It was almost four in the afternoon. Momentarily he hesitated, then poured himself a glass of sherry, searched through his CD collection until he found what he was looking for, inserted it in the player, went back to his armchair and let the strains of Mozart's piano concerto No. 21 wash over him. Maybe the music would give him the inspiration he was looking for.

As the second movement began, he tried again to remember who and where he had heard someone humming it, but the memory eluded him. He tried to imagine what sort of person could hum music like that while smashing someone's hands with a sledgehammer. They seemed to be well informed, although where they got the information that led to the arrests of Spooner and Marks was a mystery. To acquire information on the undesirable elements in the town who had already been dealt with was not really that difficult as they had all been featured in the local paper on more than one occasion. Except of course for the children. Their names would never have been published. Maybe it was a neighbour of the children who had finally decided enough was enough. After all, the neighbours would know pretty intimately what the children were like. He dismissed the idea almost immediately as very unlikely. And how could locals have been able to get information on the private lives of a senior police officer and a prominent businessman? He pulled a notebook from a drawer and began to write.

He started with what he knew from the conversations he had had with Colin Burgess and Bannerman. It wasn't much. There seemed to be at least five of them, one of whom was a woman. One was a Scot or at least had a Scottish accent, and one, maybe the same one, liked Mozart. All seemed to be oldish and one had a scar on his face. Another wore glasses. They must all be hard cases to be able to smash a man's hands, or watch it happening. Nah, this information would get him nowhere.

He tried writing down questions. Where did they get the uniforms? Where did they get a police van? Where was the building where the beatings were carried out? Why hadn't they been recognised? There were two possible answers to the last question. The first was that they are not local people. The second was that they were in disguise. Andy concluded that the disguise theory was probably the best option, but could you really disguise someone so successfully that he or she would be unrecognisable? He thought about the films he had seen. Whatever disguise the actors used playing different characters, you still always knew who they were – probably because they would want to be recognised. He needed to think about that a bit more.

Jack Templeton wasn't too happy about the name Mozart Men. He himself was known to hum or whistle classical music all the time at work and it was usually Mozart. He took some comfort from the fact that the average police officer wouldn't be able to recognise a Mozart piece even if they were informed at the start that the following music was written by that composer. Police officers like that were usually only to be found in television programmes like 'Wycliffe' and 'Morse'. Still, it was best to be sure, and it struck him that the best method of concealment was to come out into the open. So, entering the canteen when he knew it would be busy, he began to whistle the second movement of piano concerto No. 21. As he expected, someone made a remark.

"Elvira Madigan, Jack, I saw the film."

"It's Mozart, you moron. Films weren't thought of when he wrote that."

"Mozart, eh? Maybe you're this mystery man that goes round sorting out criminals like Bannerman."

"They'd get more than broken fingers if I did it," he snapped, and he drew his finger under his chin as though cutting his throat.

A number of the policemen fell about laughing and the one he knew as Tom said, "Like we told you before, Jack, you're far too soft." He turned to the others who sat round his table and added, "Anyone who lets a bluebottle out of the window rather than clobber it with a newspaper is hardly likely to swing a sledgehammer."

There was more laughter. Even Jack smiled. 'That's it,' he thought, 'just keep thinking like that.'

As he left the canteen he heard someone say, "All that time in the army – what was he, a padre?" The laughter followed him out of the room.

In his office, Inspector Burgess was looking through the file labelled the Mozart Men. The descriptions he had got from the victims had varied so much that he was convinced each one was in disguise. They had seen a moustache, a scar, a variety of hair colour, glasses, even a hearing aid. All of them could be phoney. Even the Scottish accent meant nothing. 'It's clever,' he admitted to himself. People focus on something obvious and fail to notice more important things.' He wondered why the Sharks had not given any descriptions. They had said nothing except 'We got slapped'. Were they threatened with worse if they talked? Were the others? As he sorted through the file, Constable Tate knocked and walked in.

He looked up. "Hello, Jenny."

"Sir, anything new on the Marks and Spooner case?"

Colin grinned. "You make it sound like a department store." He shuffled the papers together and added, "What I don't understand is how they got to know about their activities. I mean, Marks, of all people. A senior police officer involved in that sort of perversion." He dropped the file into a filing cabinet drawer and slammed it shut. "We have all that technology and science on our side and end up nowhere, then along come a few amateurs and BINGO, they get a result."

"How do you know they're amateurs, sir?" The Inspector looked up with a quizzical expression. "I mean, they *could* be policemen, couldn't they?" she added.

He thought for a moment. "It's possible, I suppose. I've been asked that question before but I still can't think of anyone in Church Street nick who would do anything like that."

"Maybe not, but the information they manage to get has to come from somewhere and our computers are full of it. It needn't be someone actually based here. They could just be operating from here."

He shook his head. "No, I don't buy that, Jenny. I think it has to be locals, people who are fed up with the crime rate in the area and have decided to do something about it for themselves. Unfortunately, we haven't got a clue who they are. Everything we know about them is suspect, and as for being an inside job, think about it. Both Bannerman and Spooner knew every officer in this nick, even if it was for different reasons, and if either of them had recognised one of them, we would damn well have known about it long before now."

Jenny couldn't argue with that logic. "What about this Mozart theme? Any mileage in that, do you think?"

Colin laughed. "Jack Templeton is always whistling Mozart or some such and has done for years. You can hardly suspect someone of crimes like this just because of his taste in music. All we can hope for is that they will make a mistake next time."

"Next time!"

"Oh yes. We haven't heard the last of these Mozart Men, believe me." He stood up and looked at his watch. "How good are you on the computers?"

"As good as anyone else, sir." She was actually quite an expert.

"Well, just to make sure it isn't a police officer behind all this, I want you to run a check on all the officers in Church Street and find out who was off duty at the time of the crimes. Start with the Bannerman incident. Don't forget that one of them was a woman."

"Right, sir." She left the office pleased that she seemed to have been taken seriously.

CHAPTER 17

Charles Hartley was drunk – again. He wasn't falling-down drunk, he hardly ever reached that stage, but he was argumentatively and aggressively drunk and in that state he was not a nice person to know. He had been released from prison three days earlier having served nearly two years of a three-year sentence for manslaughter – knocking down and killing an eighteen-year-old boy in Southbridge Road while more than three times over the legal limit.

He had a self-contained flat in Carley Road, which the council paid for, but no job. Charlie was not one for working. The jobs he had had in the past all ended with the sack because of his drinking habits, so now he didn't even try. As long as he could get a drink from somewhere he was content. Lack of alcohol had made prison one long nightmare for him. Withdrawal symptoms had been particularly bad, and he considered that the prison hospital had been worse than useless in dealing with them. Now he was out again and even though he had been dry for nearly two years, he'd spent the few pounds the prison service gave him on his release, on whisky. Now he was unpleasantly drunk.

He eyed the almost empty whisky bottle and wished he had another full one since he had a lot of catching up to do, but he had no money left. Remembering the pack of five cigars he had bought earlier and stowed in the top pocket of his jacket, he took one out, unwrapped it, stuck it in his mouth and patted his pockets in search of matches. He puffed vigorously on the cheap cigar sending clouds of foul-smelling smoke into the air where it hung like a fog in the small room of his flat. Coughing and spluttering he moved unsteadily across the room to open a window. Cigars were no substitute for whisky, but smoking was better than nothing. He had learnt that in the nick.

Having thought about ways to replenish his stock of alcohol, it occurred to him that his girlfriend Carol Barnard would come across for him. She always had in the past and he could see no reason why she should refuse him now. She owed him. She had his car. Admittedly he couldn't drive it, not officially anyway because he'd had a five-year ban imposed on him. He had agreed she could use it while he was in prison, but now he was out, and even though still banned from driving, he could stop her from using it – unless she paid for the privilege. Besides, he had been out for three days now and it was about time he saw her. He reckoned she would be pleased to see him. Putting his coat on against the chill of the autumn's night air, he set off for Eastley Road where she lived, a distance of some five hundred yards.

Having reached her house he banged on the door impatiently. After a moment the passage light went on and the door opened. Carol stood there, dressed ready to go out. When she saw it was Charles, she was at first disappointed and then nervous – she hadn't known he was out. The few letters he wrote to her always ended up in the bin unopened. Carol had another life now, a better one, and one that certainly did not include Charles Hartley.

The smell of whisky and cigar smoke wafted across the space between them and she looked at him with disgust. "Oh, it's you," she said, and went to close the door in his face but, drunk or not, he was too quick for her and pushed his way inside.

"I knew you would be pleased to see me, doll," he said almost jovially. He leaned forward to give her a kiss but she turned away at the smell and waved her hand in front of her face. "You're bloody drunk, Charlie," she accused. "You can't have been out five minutes and you're already pissed."

Charles raised his voice in anger and shouted at her. "I'm not pissed yet, you stupid cow, and I've run out of money." He smiled at her and lowered his voice. "But I know you'll lend me a tenner, sweetie." He patted her face in mock affection but she pushed his hand away. Peering into the front room he could see new carpet and furniture. "Looks like you've done quite well for yourself while I've been away." His face was sour.

"Things have changed, Charlie. I've got a new boyfriend now – Roy." She let her hand slide over her hip as though she were brushing out some annoying crease. "And he doesn't drink." She glared at him and added, "And I'm not lending you money to get drunk on now, or ever again. So you can push off." She reached for the door handle but he grabbed her hair and pulled hard, making her cry out.

"Well now, if you won't lend me a tenner, I'll have to bloody well take it." He dragged her into the small front room, pushed her roughly down on the settee and grabbed at her handbag, emptying the contents on the floor.

"You bastard!" she screamed, and made a desperate grab for her purse. Charlie had now become very belligerent. The money for whisky was within his grasp and he meant to have it. He lashed out with his fist, catching her full in the face and knocking her off the settee onto the floor. She lay there moaning, trying to stem the flow of blood from her nose. Opening the purse, he took the money and pocketed it. Then he noticed the car keys, *his* car keys.

"I hope you've been looking after the car, sweetie." He took the keys and dangled them in front of her. "Only I'm taking it back now." He went over to the phone, ripped it from the wall and threw it on the floor. "Just in case you get any ideas about calling the police, you bitch." He left the house slamming the front door behind him, leaving his one-time girlfriend covered in blood and crying in pain from a broken nose.

The car was kept at the back of the houses in a communal car park which used to be allotments. A gap between two houses denoted the entrance and Charlie made straight for it. It was well lit and he found the car without much difficulty. The engine roared into life at the first attempt and he called out, "First stop, off-licence!" He reversed out from the bay where it was parked, but his judgement of distance was impaired by the whisky and as he turned the wheel he caught the car next to him. The thought of stopping never entered his head and as he moved backwards a long, jagged scratch appeared all the way down the side of the other vehicle before its rear bumper was ripped off. The car careered backwards and smashed into another one parked opposite, reducing its head and rear lights to fragments. Curtains twitched as neighbours peered out to see what was going on. One or two made their way outside.

"That'll teach you to park so fucking close!" Charlie yelled to no one in particular. He pointed the car in the direction of the road and moved off. A white van was blocking his exit. Stopping the car he wound down the window and yelled, "Get that fucking van out of my way or I'll knock it out the way." The van door opened and a figure approached him. It was a policeman.

"Would you mind stepping out of the car, sir?" he asked politely.

"Yes, I would mind, sod off." The officer opened the door, grabbed Charles by the collar and pulled him out, handcuffed him and shoved him towards the waiting van.

Hartley started to shout abuse and the noise caused one or two more neighbours to appear. Carol Barnard came running out of her house. "That bastard's just attacked me and nicked my money!" she screamed. "Sixty bloody quid. It's all I've got." The woman officer climbed out of the vehicle and looked at Carol's damaged face. It was a mess.

"Did he do that?" she asked. Carol nodded. She went over to the van and returned a few seconds later with a bundle of notes which she handed over. "If you want to make a complaint for assault," she said quietly, "come to the station tomorrow. Meanwhile I'll call an ambulance. What's your name?"

Carol told the officer her name but snapped, "It's not worth making a complaint, no one will do anything till he kills some other poor sod. What he needs is a fucking good kicking."

"That's enough of that. Go back to your house and wait for the ambulance." She turned and said to the small crowd, "If anyone's car is damaged, come to the station tomorrow to report it and they'll be given a crime number. Meanwhile we have to take this man into custody as soon as possible." The onlookers nodded understandingly and agreed to inform the rest of their neighbours. The woman climbed into the back with Hartley and the van drove unhurriedly out of the street.

It never went to the station, of course. Instead it went over the river and down Southbridge Road where, after a mile or two, it turned down a narrow track and into the woods. Hartley, who had been on the floor all the while, cursed as the bumpy track caused him to keep knocking his head.

"Your driver's bloody useless," he cursed. The van slowed to a stop and the back door opened. He expected to see the lights of the police station. Instead, there was only blackness. "Where the bleeding hell are we? This ain't the police station." He peered into the gloom and could just make out the glimmer of water. He was dragged out of the van cursing wildly and dumped head first in what turned out to be a small shallow pond. Immediately he was dragged out by the feet. The water had the effect of sobering him up very quickly and he lay on his back looking up at the night sky wondering what an earth was going on. Charles Hartley was scared, very scared. He knew these people were not the police but to make sure he had to ask the question.

"What the hell are we doing here?"

One of the officers, who had been humming a tune, turned to him. "We're going to do you a favour, Charlie. We're going to stop you from drink driving. You'd like that, wouldn't you?"

"Piss off," he growled back, "you'll never stop me from drinking. I'll probably drink myself to death."

"Very likely, Charlie, and it will probably be sooner than you think, but one thing's for sure, you won't be killing any more pedestrians by driving that car of yours."

"You're not the police." He struggled to get up but a foot on his chest pushed him back down again. "What are you going to do?"

"Oh dear! We forgot that being in prison you might not have heard of us. Have you heard of John Bannerman, Charlie?"

"Bannerman?" He frowned. He tried to remember where he had heard the name. 'It must have been in prison,' he thought, 'it must have been, but who…?' It came to him. Bannerman was the one with the broken hands. He was now terrified. "What are you going to do?" he croaked. "You're not going to break my hands, are you?" His voice wavered in fear and he had a hard job not to wet himself.

"No, Charles, we're not going to do that." The officer smiled reassuringly. Hands pulled his arms over his head and secured them to the van and at the same time he could feel his legs being tied together.

"Please," he whimpered, "give me another chance. I won't drive any more, I promise."

"Sadly, we don't believe you, Charlie, so we have to make sure. You can understand that, surely?" Before he could answer he was gagged. Someone sat on his feet. Another officer approached carrying a sledgehammer. He tried to scream out 'Don't do it', but there was only a muffled sound. His head jerked from side to side and his eyes opened wide. The officer with the hammer crouched down and raised it high in the air. He was humming. As the hammer came down, Hartley screwed his eyes shut tight and tensed his whole body. The hammer smashed into his right kneecap splintering the bone with a sickening crack. He was mercifully unaware that his left knee received the same treatment seconds later.

He was bundled back into the van. The police insignia and the blue light were removed and it drove quietly back the way it had come. When they reached the spot where Hartley had run down the teenager, the van stopped. Barely conscious, he was dragged out and propped up against a tree with a notice round his neck which read.

I AM A DRUNK DRIVER AND A KILLER

THIS IS MY JUST PUNISHMENT

It was midnight before anyone noticed him.

David Matthews was driving home from a rather expensive evening out with some of the lads. The idea had been to pick up a couple of girls. but the best laid plans and even the hurriedly put together ones, often go very wrong. As he drove along Southbridge Road he turned the headlights on full beam. There was no lighting on this stretch of the road and hardly any traffic at this time of the night. Rounding a sharp left-hand bend he caught a glimpse of something or someone. By the time he realised he had seen something he had gone by, so, curiosity being what it was, he stopped the car and reversed back along the road making sure that the headlights lit up the area. When he reached the spot, he saw that it was a man propped up against a tree. There was something white on his chest. He climbed out and walked over to the sitting figure. When he saw what the notice said he realised it had to be the work of the Mozart Men. The man's legs seemed to be at funny angles and there was blood on his trousers. He walked back to the car and contacted the police on his mobile, suggesting they call an ambulance as well.

A police car arrived in less than three minutes. He saw the flashing blue light lighting up the sky long before he saw the car. Clambering out of his car as the officer approached, he pointed out where the figure of Hartley had been propped up. The officer bent down to have a good look at him, feeling his pulse to make sure he was still alive. David Matthew switched on his headlights full beam and it was then that the officer noticed the blood and the whiteness of the bone sticking through the material of the trouser legs.

"Oh shit!" he whispered and turned away. He pressed the transmit button on his radio and reported what he had seen, adding, "Is the ambulance on its way?" The voice at the other end confirmed that it was just as the siren pierced the silence of the night. The radio crackled again.

"Any idea who it is?"

"It looks very much like Charlie Hartley. We've been warned that he was out of prison and might try to use a car. From the looks of him I don't think he'll be doing any driving for a long time to come and most likely never."

The ambulance arrived and after a cursory examination they loaded him carefully aboard and sped off into the night. The officer took details from David Matthews and advised him that someone would take a statement from him the next day. David had been shocked at what he had seen, and as he drove away he remembered it was the place where an eighteen-year-old boy had been killed by a drunk driver as he walked home. He wondered if the man he had found had been the driver in question. 'Someone seems to have given him his just deserts', he reckoned.

CHAPTER 18

Colin Burgess sat at his desk holding a cup of tea. He had been looking at the crime figures for the four months from July to October and comparing them with the figures for the same time the previous year. He had noted down the information on the sheet in front of him and stared at what he had written with something like disbelief. Even though he was expecting a reduction in the figures, the results still surprised him. The trouble was, what could he do with the information? The short answer was – nothing. He couldn't make the figures public because the results would be seen as success for the vigilantes and that could easily snowball into something that would soon be out of control.

As he pondered what to do, Chief Inspector Cross came in, bringing with him an invisible cloud of cold air that seemed to swirl round him touching everything around with icy fingers. He looked frozen, and even smelled cold, a sensation that caused his brain to catapult him back to his childhood days when his mother would come home from work on a winter's day. She smelled cold, too, so very cold. Dave Cross shivered and blew air into his hands in an effort to warm them up.

"It's bloody perishing out there," he commented. "These are the days when I'm glad I can stay inside if I want to." He saw the piles of papers on the desk. "Is this the Mozart Men file? How is the investigation going?"

Colin put his hands round the now cooling cup of tea and took a gulp. "No, it's not that file and the investigation is not going very well." He heaved a sigh. "Those papers are the crime figures for the last four months and the same four months the previous year." The Chief Inspector knew there was something else to come so he waited and said nothing.

"Why are we trying to catch these people, Dave?"

"What do you mean 'why'? They're law breakers, that's why."

Colin picked up the sheet of paper he had written on and held it up. "They're law *helpers*, Dave. These people are doing us a favour. In fact they're doing everyone in Temsley a favour. These figures prove that."

"People who take the law into their own hands are not doing anyone any favours. If we start to think like that we might just as well go back to the bloody dark ages."

Colin patted the pile of papers. "These are the crime figures for the last three months. They are 20% down on the previous three months and 50% down for the same period last year. That has got to be down to them. Not only that, the clear-up rate has gone through the roof. We've got fewer unsolved crimes on our books now than at any time in the last fifteen years."

Dave Cross was shocked, and not only at the figures. He had never heard Colin Burgess express himself like that before.

"What are you saying, Colin? That we should sit back and do nothing?" His voice had a hard edge to it. "Are you saying that it's all right to smash someone's hands with a sledgehammer? What about Hartley? He's had to have both legs amputated at the knee. You call that justice?"

Colin dropped the papers back on the desk and shook his head wearily. "No, not necessarily, but neither is serving eighteen months for killing a teenager while in a drunken stupor." He stood up. "Come on, Dave," he retorted. "He was drunk last night when they stopped him from driving. He could quite easily have killed someone again."

"Makes no difference, Colin. Chopping off someone's legs is not the answer."

"Maybe not, but I'd rather see Hartley with no legs than another dead teenager."

"Your opinions aren't going to affect your ability to be objective, are they, Colin? I mean, would you rather I take you off the case?" Colin realised that he had gone too far and that he should have kept his mouth shut.

"No of course not, sir, I was just expressing a view. Even humble inspectors are allowed to have opinions."

Dave Cross tried to ease the tension by saying, "I see what you're getting at, Colin. I dare say if the truth were known, we have all felt like that at one time or another. I know I have, but that doesn't make it right."

There was a knock on the door and Jenny Tate walked in. "Oh, I'm sorry, sir," she said and made to leave.

Dave Cross called after her. "It's all right, Constable, I was just going." Jenny came back into the room, and as Dave Cross walked to the door he turned and said warningly, "Remember, it doesn't make it right." Then he was gone.

"Did I interrupt something, sir?"

"Yes, you did," he replied, "and I'm very grateful." He sat back down again and asked, "What did you get from the witnesses in Eastley Road?"

She looked gloomy. "Not a lot," she said and sighed. "Those who saw anything took no notice of appearances." She pulled her notebook out and read aloud. "'They were just police', said one. 'How can you describe a policeman in uniform?' said another. One woman said she thought one of them had an Irish accent or it could have been Scottish." She snapped the book shut. "Hartley's ex-girlfriend is in a bit of a state. He thumped her and stole the money in her purse. Mind you, one of the so-called 'officers' took it off Hartley and gave it back to her. She said she couldn't remember anything and even if she did she wouldn't tell us because, and I quote, 'the bastard only got what he deserved', unquote."

Colin nodded. He wasn't surprised at the lack of co-operation. Residents of the Eastley Estate didn't usually talk to the police. They weren't all criminals but they were frightened of reprisals. The fact that someone had told Jenny one of them had an Irish-or-possibly-Scottish accent was in itself a breakthrough, but even that was suspect. He didn't think they would ever find out who the Mozart Men were. Deep down he didn't really want to find out. They were succeeding where the police failed.

"I see the crime figures are down, sir."

Colin looked up. "Been doing your homework, have you?" he growled.

She ignored the remark. "Do you think it's because of the vigilantes?"

"Yes, I do, it has to be."

"Not the way to do it though, sir, is it? I mean breaking hands and legs is just not on."

The phone jangled noisily breaking into his train of thought and cutting off the scathing reply he was about to make. Instead, as he reached to answer it, he snapped, "Just write up your report and add it to the file." She nodded and left the office as he picked up the phone.

"Inspector Burgess."

"Colin, this is Sally." She was until very recently Marks' secretary but now she looked after the new man, Evans.

"Superintendent Evans wants to see you right away. He wants updating on the vigilante case."

"Ok, Sally, I'll be right up." He replaced the phone, collected the Mozart Men file from the cabinet and left the office.

Superintendent Roy Evans had been drafted in from the force's HQ to replace Roy Marks, who was now in custody awaiting the committal proceedings. He was an unknown quantity to Colin. He had heard rumours on the grapevine, of course, but that source of information was notoriously unreliable. Walking into the outer office Sally gave him a 'pleased to see you' smile that always made Colin feel good. He liked Sally, she was always very pleasant and never had a bad word to say about anyone.

"Hello, Sally, shall I go straight in?"

"Yes, he's expecting you."

The Superintendent looked up as he entered. He was a young man for such a senior rank, about thirty-five. He had dark hair and dark eyebrows that accentuated the smooth childlike features of his face. He peered over the top of half-moon spectacles and smiled a welcome that hinted at a perfect set of gleaming white teeth. He stood up as Colin approached and he could see that he was at least six foot four. A finger on the hand he extended wore a chunky gold ring. His wrist sported an equally chunky gold watch. His uniform was immaculate and it made Colin realise just how shabby he must look in comparison.

Evans shook hands with a firm comforting grip. "Inspector Burgess, thank you for coming so promptly," he enthused. "Being a replacement for Marks and an HQ boffin means that I need urgent updating on all the major cases on the go at the moment." He sat down, waving Colin to a chair, and for the next ten minutes or so listened intently as Colin went through the Mozart Men file.

When he had finished, he asked, "What's your opinion …er … Colin, isn't it?"

"Yes, sir," confirmed Colin. "What do you mean exactly?"

"Come on, you must have some theories, suspicions even." He fiddled with his watch strap and rubbed his wrist where it had been. "Do you think it could have been an inside job – one of our own?"

Colin replied slowly, "It's a possibility."

"You don't sound too sure."

"I'm not sir. I have been asked that question twice before and I can only give the same answer. I know every officer at this nick and I don't think any would stoop to such tactics."

"Mm … I thought I knew Roy Marks, Inspector." There was a silence. "What about someone from another station?"

"I don't think so, sir. I think it has to be someone who lives locally, perhaps someone who's been affected by crime once too often and has decided to do something about it for himself – with the help of a few others."

"That might explain one incident but not all. What about the information they seem to have?"

"Everything they know could have come from the local newspaper. It wouldn't have been difficult to find out Bannerman was a burglar or that Hartley, the latest victim, was a convicted drunk driver who had killed someone."

"The children who were beaten, *their* names would not have been in the paper."

"That's true, but the public can attend court, which is another reason why I think it's someone local."

"Or a police officer," contended Evans once again.

Colin acknowledged the point with a nod of his head.

When he left the office, he was even more convinced that it was not the work of a policeman despite the Superintendent's implying that you could never be sure about anyone. There were also twenty-six civilian staff at the station including ten traffic wardens. He suddenly remembered Jack Templeton saying, 'I know about most of the local scumbags. We also get the intelligence bulletins, you know.' That was at Charlie Slater's house in ... when was it ... June. The Bannerman incident was in July. Jack likes Mozart, everybody knew that. He suddenly realised where his train of thought was leading. 'Come on, you plonker,' he told himself, 'of all the people to suspect, Jack Templeton should be at the bottom of the list. Charlie Slater is probably worth another look. But do I want to catch them?' He shook his head and decided to ignore that last thought.

CHAPTER 19

Jack had logged into the network via the computer in the Federation's office opposite. Using Pete Allen's passwords, he once again gained access to the files that only the CID should see. He wanted information on the Oyster Night Club that had long been suspected of complicity in drug dealing. As he went through the lists, he saw the word SNARK, and knowing that the paedophile Michael Snark was due to be released from prison, he quickly printed it off. When he found the Oyster Club file he printed that off too. Having closed down the computer he picked up the papers and slipped across the corridor to his own office where he began to deal with the day's paperwork, unaware that the computer had logged the fact that the machine had been used to print off the information on Snark.

It was at home that evening, when he and Lucy had finally settled down after dinner, that they began to read the sheets he had printed. The Oyster information was very useful and he phoned Charlie to advise him that they should have another meeting at the Lion & Unicorn hotel. When he turned to the other pages he was shocked to learn that Snark was to be taken to a safe house on his release. The venue was named as Cattermole Lodge, three miles from the village of Bencham and five miles from Temsley. It was also indicated that there was new evidence connecting Snark with the murder of two children, but at the present time this had not been confirmed. Consequently, Snark was to be kept at the safe house until the hoped-for confirmation came through. He had been told that death threats against him had been received and that he was being moved for his own protection.

"What are we going to do about him?" Lucy asked.

Jack looked at her with a twinkle in his eye. "Nothing," he murmured, "absolutely nothing. But I know what I am going to do about you, young lady."

"Are you going to tell me what that is?"

"No, I'm not." He moved close to her, his arms encircling her slim figure. "I'm going to show you." His lips brushed hers and she responded with an immediacy that always surprised her.

'Why,' she wondered, not for the first time, 'have we wasted so many years before reaching this stage in our lives?' Any further thoughts were banished as Jack carried her up the stairs to the bedroom they now considered theirs.

The following evening they all met at the hotel in Ely and Jack read out the information he had obtained about the Oyster Club.

Before any discussion could take place, Lucy told them, "Jack also turned up information about Mick Snark, the paedophile." Everyone looked at Jack. He hadn't intended to bring it up just then, but he shrugged his shoulders, lit a cigarette and read out the information he had.

When he had finished, Ronnie commented, "Maybe we should go for him next. We can always come back to the Oyster Club but we won't get a second chance at this bloke."

"And what exactly do you propose to do with him? If you can get near him, that is."

"Kill the bastard," came the reply, "what else?" Although Jack was expecting it, he was shocked nonetheless at the way Ronnie had said it. So matter of fact, as though they were discussing having chicken for lunch.

"No!" said Jack firmly. "Justice is one thing, but deliberate murder? No, count me out on that one."

"Have you forgotten about Nick Baker, Jack?" Phil asked quizzically.

"No, I haven't forgotten, but once is enough. Anyway, Snark will be surrounded by police and there is no way I will take chances with the lives of police officers and neither should you." There was silence round the room.

"What about Carantel, Jack?" Charlie asked him.

Lucy, Phil, and Ronnie all looked puzzled and stared at Jack. They had never heard of the place, but Jack remembered. He remembered only too well and wished he could forget. Carantel was a village in a remote war-torn area where four rebel soldiers raped a twelve-year-old girl and then killed her. It had happened over twenty years ago but the memory was as clear in his mind as if it had happened yesterday.

"That was different, Charlie, and you know it," Jack whispered, his voice barely audible in the small room.

"The only difference was that we had guns and it was war. This is peacetime, so surely what Snark did makes it a worse crime."

Jack remembered how the young girl had screamed and sobbed but he, along with Charlie, could only watch through field glasses. When they reached the village, they were just in time to see the girl being bayoneted to death. With the same thought in both their minds, they had marched the men to the village square and made them lie on the ground. They shot each one between the legs and then in the stomach. It had taken the four of them quite a while to die. He and Charlie hadn't hesitated then. 'Those bastards deserved it.' He thought about that. Maybe Charlie was right again. Would killing Snark be so very different?

Finally he said, "If the police are anywhere near him, we don't do it. No one takes chances with innocent people." He looked round the table at each person in turn. They all nodded their agreement, including Charlie.

He glanced down at the information they had on the safe house and shook his head. "It's going to be difficult, probably impossible. Cattermole Lodge is surrounded by a ten-foot-high fence with electric sensors every few yards, so there is no way you can get over it. The front gate is electronically operated and there are CCTV cameras covering all areas." He paused to see if there were any questions or comments. "One boundary and the rear of the lodge is all open farmland, which means you can see a rabbit coming from two hundred yards. The other side is thick woods and the river. The only way you will have a chance to get at him is if he comes outside and as it's winter and bloody cold, that's hardly likely."

Ronnie spoke up. "It sounds like a non-starter already. You can't get near him so you could only shoot him. We can't do that because we don't have a gun and anyway it would alert every policeman for miles. I say we should call it off, it's far too risky."

Jack was inwardly pleased at Ronnie's contribution to the debate and was sure that everyone would agree with him.

"I have an idea about that," said Charlie. Every eye turned towards him expectantly. "We use a crossbow with a telescopic sight." Jack remembered he had been a member of an archery club during his time in the army. Charlie was confident it could be done and outlined his plan. When he had finished, no one disagreed with any part of it. It was decided that he and Jack, who as Senior Traffic Warden could arrange his days as he pleased, would go next day before Snark was taken there and confirm that the lodge was as described.

Cattermole Lodge was just as Jack had described it from the information he had obtained from the computer. It was a large, isolated house that lay some fifty yards back from the main gate down a straight drive and surrounded by high wire fences. Cutting through the wire would trigger an alarm, as would climbing over it, and because the top of the fence curved inwards, once inside there was no way back out. To the left of the house and to the rear the open farmland had nothing growing on it at all. To the right was a thick wood of mostly pine trees that ran down to the flood banks that were built up either side of the river. The road, that saw little traffic at any time, ran in front of the house past the wood and over a bridge. It turned sharp left and ran parallel to the river but was out of sight on account of the flood banks. Cameras were mounted on tall posts either side of the gate and pointing at the fence. As they drove by, Jack hoped they hadn't been caught on film.

Three days after Mick Snark arrived at Cattermole Lodge he went for a walk in the gardens. He stopped by an enormous century's old oak tree encircled by a wooden garden seat, and lit a cigarette. The officers who had been assigned to protect him were some yards away though always within sight. Neither liked the man and both were hoping the job of protecting him would not last long.

Snark sat on the garden seat facing the woods and leant back against the trunk of the oak. He was aware that the police were re-investigating the deaths of two young girls and that the 'protection for your own safety' was just a ruse to keep him in one place while they tried to secure evidence. He was certain they would not obtain that evidence. He remembered the two girls vividly and had no conscience about them. What he did, he enjoyed, and he was always very careful to cover his tracks. He could think of nothing that would link him to their murders. His capture had been purely accidental – a case of being in the wrong place at the wrong time. He was convinced the police had nothing at the moment otherwise they would have arrested him, but he had heard the rumours on the prison grapevine and that was usually reliable. It could have been a wind-up as he was shunned by other prisoners. They might have started the rumours just to rile him, knowing that he was due for release. For now he was content to bide his time and enjoy the limited freedom he had.

Charlie Slater had been unable to believe his luck when he had seen Snark walking in the garden. He had been coming to this spot for three days now, at various times, and today he had to leave by 14:50 hours in order to be back at the car by 15:00. It would take him eight minutes to complete the short journey through the woods, cross the river and be on the other side where Jack's car would be waiting. It wouldn't go without him, of course, but they knew that a small bus came up the road at 15:10 every day and it was imperative they weren't noticed.

He loaded the crossbow and peered through the telescopic sights. He watched as Snark lit a cigarette and sat down facing the woods. It was an invitation almost too good to be true. A glance in the direction of the guards told him they were at least thirty yards away from Snark. He lined up the sights on his quarry's neck, knowing the bolt would sever the spinal column before it embedded itself in the tree. Snark seemed to be looking straight at him as he gently squeezed the trigger. It took less than twenty seconds to aim and fire and he knew his aim had been right on target.

Snark thought he saw a movement in the trees and looked towards it. There was a soft 'whooshing', a momentary pain in his neck, and he was dead. He never heard the dull thud of the bolt as it buried itself in the trunk of the tree he was leaning against and there was no time to cry out. The two officers heard nothing, only saw that Snark was still leaning against the tree. They did not see the figure of Charlie Slater as he climbed down from his observation post, pausing only to leave the white card that said:

PAEDOPHILE CHILD KILLER. JUSTICE HAS BEEN DONE

and neither did they hear him as he made his way back to the river.

Charlie reached the river bank and glanced at his watch. Seven minutes to 3 o'clock, plenty of time. Dropping the crossbow into the inflatable dinghy he had left on the bank, he slid it into the water and paddled swiftly across. When he reached the other side he dragged it out, pulled the plugs, and while the air was still escaping hoisted it rapidly up the flood bank. Peering over the top of the bank, he could see Jack standing near the back of the car. The road was clear so he scrambled down, pulling the deflating dinghy with him. Jack had already opened the boot. The dinghy was thrown in along with the crossbow, and covered with a blanket. Both men climbed into the car and it pulled unhurriedly away and headed towards Wisbech.

Up to this point neither man had spoken. "He's dead," said Charlie breathlessly. "He sat on a garden bench by a tree and 'wham' he was dead. The guards were thirty yards away at least and never heard a thing. I bet they still don't know."

Jack said nothing. The job done, he drove to the car park they had chosen on the edge of Wisbech, opened the boot and pushed the deflated dinghy into a large heavy-duty plastic sack. Building work was in progress in the yard adjoining the car park and a half-empty skip stood adjacent to the car park wall – the reason for choosing that particular spot. The plastic sack disappeared into it and they drove away. No one had seen them arrive and no one saw them leave, and even if they had, no one would have taken any notice. As they drove back to Temsley, Charlie dismantled the weapon. The pieces were scattered into the river. It was unlikely they would ever be found.

Pulling into the Leisure Centre car park, Jack removed the one-piece overall he was wearing. Leaving his car he walked the few yards to the rear of the police station and made his way to the canteen. He saw Colin Burgess coming toward him.

"It's all right for some people," said the Inspector as he hurried by.

The officers could see that Snark was still sitting by the tree. One said, "Should I see if he's all right? He's been sitting out there for quite a while and it's pretty cold."

"No," said the other, "leave him. I don't care if the bastard catches pneumonia." Another ten minutes passed.

"I'm going to take a look. He might be sleeping, or he might be ill." The other shrugged his shoulders, took a pipe from his top pocket and began to fill it with tobacco from his leather pouch, tamping it down with his thumb.

As the guard approached the oak tree he called out, "Snark! Are you all right?" There was no answer and no movement. His head was down as though he was asleep. The officer bent forward and shook his shoulder. The head lolled over to one side revealing a large blood stain and the bolt that had gone through his throat and pinned his neck to the tree. The officer went white. "Oh Jesus," he whispered, then turned away and vomited.

At the same time this was happening at Catermole Lodge, Jack was in his office and Charlie was selling a car in his showroom. Charlie had been jubilant, but Jack was getting worried. Where would it all stop? They couldn't carry this sort of thing on indefinitely.

CHAPTER 20

Roy Evans was fuming. He stood at his window and stared across the frost-tinged grass to the river. The trees were naked of any greenery now and their branches pointed skywards like burnt blackened fingers. Normally the view of the river would have had a calming effect on him but today the sight made his anger burn even brighter. He continually rubbed at his wrist where his watch strap left indentations on his skin.

Snark was dead. Despite all the precautions and the secrecy surrounding his release and transfer to the safe house, he was dead. A crossbow bolt in the throat, how very William Tell. What made it worse, if it could get any worse, was that Andy Mills, the Mozart Men's chosen one, had received the predictable notification and despite the police having refused to confirm that anything had happened, had said he would publish the story regardless, something like 'I have received information which states …,' thus indicating that the Mozart Men were responsible.

"Bloody Mozart Men," he said aloud. "Bloody stupid title. They're vigilantes, murderers." The phone buzzed on his desk forcing him to control his fury. He picked up the phone and was immediately composed. "Superintendent Evans."

It was the Chief Constable. He wanted a full report by lunchtime at the latest on progress in catching the vigilantes. He also informed Evans that there was to be a full inquiry into how a safe house had become common knowledge. Security had to be tightened up with immediate effect. After replacing the phone, Evans wondered how he could possibly tighten up security in an area that should already be watertight. "It'd be like trying to tighten a nut that's already at its limit," he muttered to himself. Opening the office door he called to his secretary, "Get Inspector Burgess up here, will you, Sally. Tell him to drop whatever he's doing and call him in if he's out!" She nodded and reached for her phone.

Colin sat at his desk drinking a cup of the filthy liquid that passed for tea, or was it coffee, that he had got from the canteen machine. He was expecting the call and was ready when the telephone suddenly came to life.

"He wants to see you, Colin. He's had a call from the Chief and he's not very happy," she warned.

"Thanks for the tip off, Sally, I owe you a drink."

She laughed.

"I prefer chocolates," she quipped.

Replacing the phone, he dropped the plastic cup containing whatever it was into the bin and picked up the file, complete with the latest reports on the Snark killing, although he didn't think he would have any answers to the questions he knew Evans was going to ask. One thing was certain though, he could discount any thoughts he might have had about Jack Templeton being involved – he had been in his office when the balloon went up and he was pretty certain Jack had never held a crossbow in his life.

"I have been instructed to tighten security," snapped Evans as Colin sat himself in the chair opposite. The Superintendent had been dragged over the coals and he was going to make sure he passed some of that on. "Who had access to the Snark file?"

"Security is pretty tight, sir, and only CID had access to the Snark information – apart from all the senior officers from Superintendent upwards." Evans thought he detected a hint of sarcasm but apart from a sharp look he ignored it. Colin continued, "Anyway, the computer will have logged everyone who accessed the information on Snark."

Evans looked up quickly. "You mean there is a list of people who have accessed the Snark file?"

"Yes, sir. Complete with date, logging on and logging off time and the workstation number."

"Who is on that list?"

"Not sure yet, sir. That information can only be supplied by the IT department."

"Well, get on to it, man, I want a copy on my desk pronto." He rubbed at his wrist and Colin wondered why he didn't simply loosen the watch strap. "What about civilian staff? Have any of those got access?"

"No, sir, none."

Evans continued as though he hadn't heard what his Inspector had just said. "Secretaries, typists, anyone?"

"No, sir, no one."

"In that case, Inspector, it must be a police officer."

"With all due respect, sir, we haven't actually established that the information was leaked from here or that it came off *our* computer system. There must be others who had the information."

Evans stared at him across the desk as though unable to believe what he had just heard. "Only the top-ranking officers in this force and the prison governor knew of the arrangements," he said coldly, "unless of course you want to accuse the Home Secretary. Other than that, it is as you say – only the CID had access."

Colin didn't argue, he couldn't. He was convinced that hackers couldn't access the system from outside, and civilians on the inside didn't have the passwords needed. Logically it had to be a police officer, but despite the evidence he decided to reserve judgement until he had the list.

When he got back to his office the e-mail from the IT department was waiting for him. He printed off two copies and deleted the message. There were four names on the list. Two were Chief Superintendents and one was Chief Inspector Cross. It was the last one that interested him – DC Peter Allen. The list had the date, times, and workstation number. He checked the number against the list and discovered it was located in an office that had originally been listed to the Federation but was now going to be made available to the newly formed Family Unit. It was at the moment empty, and he was shocked to discover that the workstation was still connected to the computer network. The IT department should have cancelled the connection.

He put one of the lists in an envelope and sealed it, then, going into the main CID office he told the nearest person to take it up to the Superintendent's office. Standing at the door he called out, "Pete, my office, now."

Pete looked up, rather surprised.

Two of the other officers grinned. "Who's been a naughty boy?" said one.

"What you been up to, Pete?" asked another.

Pete just shrugged his shoulders and raised his eyebrows.

When he entered the office he was told to shut the door. He was not invited to sit down and that was a sign that usually meant trouble. He waited for the Inspector to speak.

"Why did you access the Snark file, Pete?"

Pete was taken aback. "The Snark file?" he repeated.

"Yes. Don't play games with me, Pete. What did you want that information for?"

"I haven't accessed the file," protested Pete, "I've had no reason to."

"Really? Well, the computer says different."

Pete, like everyone else at the nick, knew that Snark was dead and realised the implication of what was being said. "Now hold on, Guv, I haven't been near the Snark file and I don't care what the computer says."

Colin was inclined to believe him but the evidence was pretty conclusive. "Who else knows your passwords?"

"No one as far as I'm aware, except maybe the people in the IT department."

Colin shook his head. "No, they don't know your passwords or anyone else's, only the default ones."

The phone rang and Colin snatched it up. "Inspector Burgess." He listened, then nodded down the phone. "Yes, sir, he's with me now." There was another pause and another "Yes, sir," and finally, "Very good, sir." He sat there looking at the phone in his hand as though trying to decide what to do with it.

"That was Evans." He dropped the phone back on its receiver. "He wants to see you about this matter right away."

"In that case," declared a very worried Pete, "I want a Federation rep with me. I want witnesses to any accusations he throws my way."

"That's your right," conceded Colin. Pete turned to go. "If it's any consolation, Pete, I believe you."

The detective constable jerked his thumb at the ceiling. "Let's hope he does."

Colin put his elbows on the desk and rested his head in his hands. "Oh shit," he whispered, "what a bloody mess."

Half an hour later there was a knock on the door. Before he could respond, the door opened and Jack Templeton stuck his head round it. "Got a minute?" he asked.

Colin waved him in. "What can I do for you, Jack?"

"I've just seen Pete Allen," Jack said, "says he's been suspended, something about Snark."

"Come on, Jack, I can't discuss that with you."

Jack held up his hand. "I know that, but surely you don't suspect him of having killed Snark?"

"No of course I don't." He pulled a packet of mints from his pocket, took one and offered the tube to Jack, who shook his head. "But someone has been giving information out. The computer says he accessed the file and he says he didn't."

"You mean you actually believe he's been giving out information?" Jack's tone was accusatory.

"It doesn't matter what I believe. The computer registers everyone who accessed the Snark file and his name is on the list." He stood up, "Look, I've said too much already."

Jack was thoughtful. He liked Pete, a good copper with nearly thirty years' service. He wasn't going to let him take the blame if he could help it.

"Is that what this is about? Information off a computer?"

"Jack!"

"No, hear me out. I've got a computer in my office. Now I don't know much about them but I could have got that information."

Colin shook his head. "Nice try, Jack, but it won't wash. You would need his passwords, and he assures me that no one else knows them."

Jack frowned and decided to take a chance. "Do you think I know *your* passwords, Colin?"

The Inspector frowned. "No, you don't. What are you getting at?"

"I'm trying to tell you that passwords are a joke and I would like to bet that anyone who knows Pete quite well, away from work that is, would be able to figure out his passwords. Now I don't know Pete socially, but I know you quite well and I'm telling you I could work out your passwords."

Colin looked sceptical. Eventually he said, "All right, try it, but I won't tell you if you're right."

When Jack left the office ten minutes later he left a very shocked CID Inspector behind him. Jack had correctly identified two of his passwords and, using the same logic, would have almost certainly been able to work out his password made up of numbers. He had thought his passwords were foolproof and only now did he realise how stupid they were. He shuddered involuntarily when he realised it could so easily have been his passwords someone used and not Pete's. With this came another realisation that chilled his blood. It was really beginning to look as though at least one of the Mozart Men was a police officer. He remembered saying to Evans, 'Security is pretty tight'.

"That's a laugh," he said aloud, "security is a bloody joke. But I'll soon alter that."

CHAPTER 21

Colin Burgess acted immediately and security was tightened with dramatic effect. The computer in the empty office was removed and the door kept locked. It was a bit like locking the stable door after the horse had bolted but it was hoped that it would send a message to whoever was responsible for the information leak. He still couldn't believe it was someone at the station and was convinced that somehow, someone on the outside had managed to hack into the system.

Jack was relieved when he discovered that Pete's suspension had been lifted, although it had nothing to do with his little chat to Inspector Burgess – it was confirmed that at the time he was supposed to have been on the computer, he was in fact having an x-ray at the local hospital. Still, he knew that his chat to Colin must have come pretty close to the truth when the caretaker removed the computer from the office opposite and locked the door. He dared not try getting information using his own office machine, not now. Anyway, he was certain that the passwords would all have been altered and that any new ones would be random and not linked to something that was easy to remember.

A part of him was relieved that he would not be able to access the files. The new security clamp-down would make it difficult to continue being vigilantes and dishing out their own special brand of justice, although on the other hand, there were still the Intelligence Bulletins and often there would be photos of local villains that the police wanted to interview, or wanted a special eye kept on. Deep down he hoped that the others would decide to call it a day. Or to be more precise, he hoped that Lucy would.

His relationship with Lucy had developed beyond his wildest dreams. Far from rejecting him, she loved him with an intensity that he never thought possible. He knew of course, that people could love one another with a passion that burned like fire, but he never ever dreamed that someone would love *him* that way. Just to think of her set his heart racing and his head swimming. He had made up his mind to ask her to marry him but there was still a niggling little doubt in the back of his mind that she might think it too early for that sort of a commitment, after barely six months. The thought of her turning him down was something he didn't want to think about. Despite that, he still intended to ask her. He reflected how much he had changed since their love affair had bloomed.

Apart from his relationship with Lucy, which thankfully Charlie was very pleased about, he had been feeling increasingly unwell. Headaches, nausea, and chest pains had left him tired and without appetite, although it hadn't stopped him smoking. He had been unable to hide the symptoms from Lucy and, although he made light of them, he had taken her advice and made an appointment to see the doctor. He wasn't too keen to visit civvy street doctors although he had never actually been to see one. He was pretty sure they would say 'Stop smoking and stop drinking'. At one time he would have said that, if he had to do that he might as well stop living, but now of course there was Lucy to consider. He glanced at his watch: 10:45. His appointment was for 11o'clock. Time to go and hear the worst.

He put his head round the station sergeant's door. "I'm just going to see the MO, Trevor, I won't be long."

Trevor looked up in surprise. "You?" he exclaimed, "Going to see a doctor? Nothing serious, I hope."

Jack shrugged. "Shouldn't think so, more of a check-up than a problem really. See you later." He pulled on an overcoat and a scarf against the chill wind. Once outside, he lit a cigarette before setting off on the ten-minute walk. An hour later he was making his way back to the office clutching a letter for the hospital. He had been pleasantly surprised at the attitude of the doctor who, although asking him if he smoked, did not tell him to give it up but commented instead, 'It doesn't help these types of symptoms'. Similarly, when he told him about his drinking habit the doctor's comment had been, 'Whisky, in moderation of course, won't do any harm'. After a thorough examination the doctor had stated that he wasn't sure what was wrong and more tests were in order. He had picked up the phone and managed to make an appointment at the hospital for that afternoon.

Going back into the station he put his head round Trevor's door again. It was the sergeant who spoke first. "Everything all right, Jack?"

"Yes, fine, but I have to go for some tests at the hospital this afternoon."

"This afternoon?" Trevor cried in disbelief. "What did you do, threaten him with parking tickets, or are you in the know?"

"In the know? I wish. Apparently there was a cancellation so they fitted me in instead."

"Lucky you."

The phone rang and the sergeant answered it, waving his hand in a goodbye gesture as Jack left.

Jack was apprehensive about the hospital appointment. The doctor hadn't said what he thought the problem was, just that there were no immediate signs of certain things that he might have expected. Jack assumed that if he didn't know, it couldn't be anything serious, so he had accepted the recommendation to have further tests. He wondered, though, why he should have got an appointment so quickly when the newspapers were full of stories about patients waiting weeks for a consultation. The fact that he hadn't seen a doctor since leaving the army might have had something to do with it, but nonetheless he still thought it unusual. Then again, maybe he just got lucky with a cancelled appointment.

He sat in his office trying to sort out his mail, but the headache that had started earlier showed no signs of abating. He suddenly felt very sick and almost had to run to reach the toilet in time. He remembered years ago someone in his unit having headaches and being sick and recalled that he was suffering with appendicitis. He decided he must be suffering from that too, and for some reason the thought made him feel better. He picked up the phone and dialled his home number. Lucy answered.

"Hello, sweetheart, it's only me."

"Jack – how did it go at the doctors? Is everything all right?"

"Yes, but I think I've got appendicitis. The doctor has sent me to the hospital for tests."

"The hospital! Where are you now?"

"In my office. The appointment isn't until 3 o'clock."

"Right," she declared, "I'll pick you up about twenty-to, so be ready."

"Don't worry, love, I'll walk there. It's only ten minutes."

"You'll do no such thing," she scolded. "Look, Jack, if it's what you think it is, then walking is the last thing you should be doing."

He didn't want to argue with her. "All right," he said, "I'll see you then." He looked at his watch: 12:30. He didn't feel like eating but he leaned over and took his flask and sandwiches from his bag. After he had poured himself a cup of black coffee it occurred to him that if it was his appendix they would want to operate and that would mean he shouldn't have anything to eat or drink. Reluctantly he poured the coffee back into the flask and replaced it along with his sandwiches back in the bag. At 2:30 he made his way down to the yard. Lucy was already there, her eyes firmly fixed on the back door, waiting for him to appear. He smiled and waved to her then climbed into the passenger seat.

"You certainly look a bit washed out," she observed. "Why didn't you go to the doctor's sooner?"

He shrugged his shoulders. "I didn't want to worry you. Anyway, it's probably nothing, might not even be appendicitis."

The idea that it might be nothing did not sit well with Lucy. The fact that he had gone to the doctor in the first place meant it was serious. The car moved off and she pulled out into the main road to begin the short journey, made in silence, up the Mallerton road to the hospital. Parking the car as near to the hospital entrance as she could get, she searched her handbag for coins to put in the ticket machine.

"Look, Lucy, there's no need for you to stay. I don't know how long this will take."

She looked up sharply with a determined look on her face. "I don't care how long it takes, Jack, I'm staying." She climbed out of the car and went to buy a ticket. Jack was secretly relieved that she wanted to stay. He was constantly amazed at her love for him and still, at times, found it hard to understand.

The wind was cold and it had started to drizzle as they made their way to the main entrance. Having found out from a smiling and helpful lady at the enquiry desk just where to go, they set off down the maze of corridors making sure to follow the signs. He reported his presence to the nurse at the desk and sat down with Lucy on a long, soft-cushioned bench. There were three other people waiting, two men and a woman. One man was staring out of the window, the other was reading a newspaper which he shook every so often in order to straighten the pages, causing the woman who was reading a paperback book to stare at him and tut in annoyance. Jack tried to read the title of her book but all he could see was a picture of a couple in an embrace on the cover.

He didn't have long to wait even though they were early, and Lucy watched as he disappeared into another room, her lips clenched together with anxiety.

Thirty minutes later a nurse enquired, "Mrs Templeton?" Lucy looked up and was going to correct the error but thought it had such a nice ring to it she decided to let the nurse think she was right.

"Yes?"

"Have you got transport?"

"Yes – is everything all right?" There was more than a hint of alarm in her voice.

"Oh yes," the nurse assured her, "he's still a bit groggy after the tests, but he's fine. Get him home and put him to bed, the rest will do him good." A porter appeared pushing Jack in a wheelchair. He certainly looked decidedly muzzy but there was an air about him that told the world he was not happy at being treated like an invalid.

The porter, a cheerful chap, smiled and said, "If you bring the car to the front entrance we'll be waiting for you." Lucy hurried off.

The following morning, Jack reluctantly decided that a day off was called for and asked Lucy to phone in for him. She was pleased, not that he was poorly, but that he was acting sensibly and not trying to be 'macho'. She had expected him to struggle into work whether he was feeling well or not. A dark thought flitted into her mind – 'If he's willing to have a day off it means he must be worse than I thought. Whatever is wrong with him it is definitely not appendicitis.'

The tightening of security by Colin Burgess, coupled with the fact that Jack still wasn't feeling so good, meant that there was a lull in the activities of the Mozart Men. Jack had, however, soon gone back to work despite feeling decidedly unwell at times, and as a result he still managed to get some information from the Intelligence Bulletins, but it was limited to minor offences.

"I don't think we should stop altogether just because of me," he told Lucy as they settled down on the settee after dinner one evening. "Someone might put two and two together, especially as they're now convinced the information is coming from the inside." Lucy nodded. She could see the logic to that statement. He waved a sheet of paper. "The two lads here should be no problem. Petty thieves and vandals the pair of them, but they need to be taught a lesson. The leather strap should sort them out."

"All right," Lucy agreed, "but you're not going." She paused before adding. "We can't go on indefinitely with this, not with you unwell and this security business at the station. They'll probably be watching everyone now, though I don't think they'll track us down." Jack nodded in agreement. It looked very much as though their activities were about to come to an abrupt end and he was thankful. Enough was enough. They had made a difference, he knew that, but now it was time to stop.

CHAPTER 22

It was December, just a few short weeks to Christmas and the start of another year, a year closer to his retirement. Andy Mills had continued to give the Mozart Men a lot of thought but, like the police, couldn't come up with any answers. The police had more information, such as the statements from those who had been their victims, statements he was not privy to. All he had managed was a chat to Bannerman and a few words with Amanda Green and Wendy Miles, neither of whom had been eager to tell him anything. Maybe they told the police nothing, maybe they were too frightened to say anything. It would go a long way to explain the failure of the police to catch them.

He paced round his living room with a large glass of sherry in his hand. When he had finished this one, he would have another. After all, he had nowhere to go at eight o'clock on a cold December night. 'Vigilantes,' he thought, 'I remember a few in the past that I wrote stories about, but none of them was as organised as this lot.' He recalled a number of cases where people had tried to imitate police officers, all for different reasons, but he could not remember a single case where *one* person had dressed as a policeman and drove a police van, let alone four or five. Just how many of them were there?

He crossed the room, selected a CD at random and inserted it in the player, then eased himself into his favourite chair. The music of Mozart once more filled the air and he smiled and said loudly, "Very appropriate really, maybe I'll be on the suspect list next."

As the music swirled round the room he found it enabled him to think better. Whoever it was clearly had access to information about criminals, including vandals and young tearaways, information that was in plentiful supply at a police station. They would also need access to a police van or one they could dress up and pass off as such. They would need false number plates too, or the means to make them up. Then there were the uniforms, radios, and the other equipment that policemen carried such as handcuffs. Knowledge of Temsley would be high on the list of 'must haves' and they also had to have somewhere to take their victims. A thought struck him. He switched on his video player and inserted the tape of the Sharks getting their comeuppance.

Although he studied it very carefully there wasn't much to see. The camera was focused purely on the punishment that was taking place. Even so, the more he thought about it the more he began to think it was some sort of factory unit. There were plenty of those around. New ones were being built all the time and standing empty for long periods, and even the old ones had a fair turnover of clients as more and more small firms went to the wall. The Sharks were walloped during the day, so if it was a factory unit then it would have to be a new one that no one had yet moved into. Even with a new development there would be builders around unless it was completely finished and completely empty. He resolved to look at some of them the following day.

All of a sudden, Jack Templeton came to mind, the man in charge of a team of traffic wardens. It was he who he had heard humming or whistling Mozart. Now then, *he* would have access to information – but police uniforms and equipment? Well, maybe, but it was a very big maybe. What about a police van? That had to be a no. There was no way he would be able to borrow a police van, there were too many risks involved in that even if he could get the keys, and that was doubtful. Mind you, he was a mate of Charlie Slater and *he* owned a garage and a showroom. If he sold the type of vans the police used, that could answer one part of the question. The question was, would Charlie Slater be involved in something like that? He wondered how far the pair of them went back. If they were both involved, then the one thing they would have to be able to do was trust one another and that sort of trust usually meant a long-term friendship. A few discreet enquiries would not go amiss.

What else would they need? A motive, certainly – they must have a motive. No one would do this sort of thing without a motive and it would have to be very compelling too. What sort of motive would you need to break someone's hands or legs. He remembered that Charlie Slater had his house burgled back in the summer but would that be a good enough motive? No, doubtful that, unless it was the last straw and that would mean that something else had happened to him or even his family. That needed to be checked as well.

There was also at least one woman involved. Who was she, why was she with them, and why was it none of them was ever recognised? Even with a wig or a false moustache, the person underneath is usually recognisable. You only had to go to the pictures or watch the television to realise that. Some of the victims wouldn't know those responsible even if they weren't disguised, but locals like Hartley or Bannerman would know practically all the policemen in the local station, at least by sight. Come to that, so would Jeff Spooner, so it was unlikely to be a police officer.

Superintendent Marks would have known every person in the station but the Mozart Men didn't visit him. Was that because they just passed on the information about him, or was it because they were worried they would have been recognised? He poured himself another large sherry and resolved to give the whole thing a rest until the morning. Decision made, he changed the CD and settled down to listen to some more music, only this time it was jazz.

The following day, Andy looked up the copies of the newspapers for June. He soon found the story about Charlie Slater's house being burgled and smashed up. The only things missing were some items of jewellery which were never recovered, even though two men, known drug addicts, were arrested for the crime.

As he pored over the microfiche film a female voice enquired, "What are you looking for, Andy, can I help?" He looked up to see Gladys, who had been with the newspaper for over thirty-five years and was a vital source of information about the files and the stories the paper had covered.

"Hello, Gladys." He smiled at her and not for the first time thought how attractive she was. Middle fifties with the figure of a teenager, well almost, always cheerful and never a bad word to say about anyone. "I was just looking up the Slater burglary."

She nodded. "I remember that. June last year, smashed the place up but stole only a handful of jewellery. Two addicts were arrested but the jewellery was never recovered." She never ceased to amaze him with her knowledge.

"That's the one. I don't know how you remember everything so clearly."

She flushed with pleasure at the compliment. "That one was easy," she replied. "I'm a friend of Kate Ellis, Charlie Slater's housekeeper, and she said it was a terrible mess. Everything was smashed, even their crystal glasses. I felt really sorry for Mr

Slater when I heard about it, especially after his previous upset."

Andy perked up at hearing this. "Oh, what upset was that?"

"Couple of years ago it was." She touched the side of her face with three fingers. "His wife and child were killed on a zebra crossing by a teenager in a stolen car. As I recall, he was a drug addict as well."

Andy snapped his fingers. "Of course! I remember that now." He gave Gladys a kiss on the cheek. "Gladys, you're a real treasure." He headed for the door, suddenly thought of another question, and turned back to her. "I don't suppose you know how long Charlie Slater and Jack Templeton have been friends?"

"You mean that nice traffic warden? Course I do. They both grew up around here and were in the army together. We did a lot of stories about them, you know – Ireland and such, even the Falklands, a couple of local heroes they were."

"Thank you, Gladys, thank you very much. I'll buy you a drink sometime."

"I'd prefer a night of passion," she called out as Andy fled through the door. Unfortunately, he didn't hear her.

Andy spent the rest of the morning driving round all the industrial sites and business parks in Temsley, but there were none that he thought could be where the vigilantes carried out their punishments. There were plenty of empty factory units but they all had occupied premises next door, or opposite, sometimes both. There was no way that the beatings could have taken place in any of them. People would have seen a police van. It would have been very conspicuous. He was about to give up the idea as a wild goose chase when he remembered that there was a new business park being built south of the river.

He drove through the town and over the river bridge opposite the fire station. After about two miles he saw a sign pointing to the right which read TEMSLEY & DISTRICT BUSINESS PARK. He turned down the lane and soon found himself surrounded by brand new factory units, none of which, as far as he could tell, were occupied. There were three roads all linked together and he drove down all three but didn't see a soul. He stopped the car, and pulling his coat tightly round him against the chill of the biting wind, walked along the line of buildings, peering in through some of the windows and checking doors for any sign of entry, but he could see nothing.

As he walked back to his car, a security van turned into the road driving slowly along the line of buildings. When the driver noticed Andy he stopped and got out.

"Have the agents sent you?" he asked in what Andy thought was a 'county' accent.

"The agents?"

"Yes, Brindley's."

"No. No one sent me. I came to look round but none of them seem to be occupied. How long have they been finished?"

The security man looked Andy up and down, trying to decide if he could be trusted. Glancing from side to side he said in a low voice. "They've been finished about six months. There's been a few people come to look at them but, well, to be honest, they're far too expensive for round here. There's no call for them, see, especially when there's all them empty ones nearer the town, and cheaper too." Andy nodded in agreement.

"Yes, I saw most of those this morning. Who were the people who looked at these ones, do you know?"

The guard shook his head. "No. We're only employed to look at them and make sure there's no damage."

He looked round and lowered his voice even further. "Mind you, we only come once in daylight and once at night, so if the local louts wanted to cause damage they'd have plenty of time."

Andy walked back to his car and unlocked it. "You say the agents are Brindley's?"

"Yes, that's right, opposite the bus station."

Andy thanked him and got into his car.

"Don't go paying their rates though," yelled the guard, "And you tell them this ain't London."

Andy raised his hand and drove slowly away. Things were beginning to take shape in his mind. Maybe the Mozart Men weren't as clever as everyone thought. He parked the car in the long-stay car park opposite the Windmill pub, crossed the High Street and walked down to the Mercury Shopping Centre. He had remembered to pick up his hat, a checked one with a coloured feather in the band, but had forgotten his gloves, so he thrust his hands deep into his pockets against the cold. Brindley's was situated on the outside of the shopping complex facing the street, and looked too large for an estate agents, even an upmarket one like theirs that dealt exclusively in properties over 200k. If the property wasn't worth six figures or more it wouldn't be on Brindley's books, which was why Andy was surprised that the factory units were theirs.

He pushed open the door and stepped in. The heat hit him like a brick wall. He stood for a moment taking in his surroundings. The carpet was deep pile, the lighting hidden and the furniture all top of the range. 'None of those desks ever saw the inside of MFI,' he thought. He glanced at some photographs of properties for sale while trying to decide how to ask the questions he wanted answers to without sounding too inquisitive.

His thought processes hadn't got to first base before a female voice said, "Good morning, Mr Mills, can I help you?"

Andy looked up, surprised that someone working here

would know his name, a fact that put paid to any white lies he might have been going to tell. The woman addressing him was tall and elegant, a stunner in every way.

"Good morning, do I know you?" he asked, wishing fervently that he did. The woman smiled, showing gleaming white teeth.

"You covered the fête at Mallerton Hall in June. I was the organiser."

Andy searched his memory and a name popped up. "Mrs Tinsley?" he queried. "You look, er, different." He remembered her as wearing blue jeans and a tee-shirt, a far cry from the immaculately dressed figure that stood before him now.

She smiled again. "Well, that was rather a casual dress day." She raised her eyebrows questioningly. "What can we do for you, Mr Mills?"

He paused and then decided to plunge right in. "I hear you are the agents for the Temsley & District Business Park."

"Oh! Where did you hear that?" She said it as though she was reluctant to discuss the Business Park.

He decided to risk a little white lie. "Charlie told me, said he was interested in having one of the units."

She raised her eyebrows again. "Charlie?" Clearly she wasn't keen to know anyone with such a common name.

"Yes, you know, from the showroom up the road."

Her features registered recognition. "Oh, you mean Charles Slater. Yes, he did show an interest but I understand they were not what he had in mind."

"You've given him a tour, then?"

"Tour? No, we gave him a key and he took himself round. What, may I ask, is your particular interest in those er, units?"

He had to risk another white lie. "The Gazette is considering moving to different premises – our current accommodation is really too small. Renting one of those units might be a good move."

Mrs Tinsley chuckled softly. "We are not in the renting business, Mr Mills. Those units are for sale."

'So that's why Brindley's are dealing with them,' thought Andy. Aloud he said, "Ah, that puts a different light on the matter, I'm afraid. I doubt the paper would want to buy. They would be expensive no doubt?"

"They do come within the guidelines we set for all the properties we deal with, yes."

Andy nodded and turned towards the door, pulling it open. "Thank you for your time." He stepped into the cold, windswept street, somehow relieved at being away from a business whose cheapest prices were two hundred grand.

A look at his watch told him it was one o'clock and the gurgling in his stomach informed him he was hungry. Looking across the High Street he saw the newest pub in town, The Monk. The front was all plain glass and within he could see the tastefully decorated bar and people enjoying hot meals. It looked very inviting and although it was undoubtedly expensive, he decided to give it a try. The only other pub nearby was the Windmill and he didn't fancy that.

It was surprisingly quiet for a lunchtime and he had no difficulty finding a corner table well away from the door. He ordered a non-alcoholic lager and a shepherd's pie, and as he waited for his meal he sipped his drink and reflected on what he had found out. Pulling a notebook from his pocket he began to write. At the top of the page he wrote KNOWN, and underneath he wrote:

CS Wife and child killed by drug addict in stolen car

CS House smashed up by drug addicts in June
CS and JT good friends and old army pals
JT has access to information
CS had had keys to factory unit on a completely empty site
Security checks at park once during day and once at night

On another page he wrote QUESTIONS and underneath:

Could JT get police equipment?
Does CS sell vans of the type the police use?
Did CS have extra keys to the unit cut?
How many vigilantes are there?
Who is the woman?
Why haven't they been recognised? Makeup artist?

His lunch arrived, so he pocketed his notebook and began to eat, wondering as he did so who would know about makeup. He finally decided on his friend Vivien, who ran the Amateur Dramatic Society. He would certainly know whether it was possible to make someone up so that they were completely unrecognisable. He finished his meal – not quite worth the cost – and made his way to Vivien's home.

Vivien was a man of some considerable means and lived in the last house, which was more like a small mansion, in Mallerton Road, opposite the college. He had moved there after a lifetime's career in the theatre where he had worked at every job going, including acting and directing. Public appearances for him were now a thing of the past but he liked to keep occupied with 'Amdram' as he called it.

The front door, with its lion's head knocker, was rather imposing and Andy knocked on it expecting to hear the lion's head roar, rather than the hollow 'clunk' that echoed round the house. The happy sound of a man singing was heard and then the door swung open. Vivien stood there in blue jeans and the most colourful tee-shirt that Andy had ever seen. There was no pattern, just an explosion of colour. Despite being nearly seventy he showed no signs of going grey, which made Andy instantly suspect hair colouring or a wig. If it was the latter, it was an excellent one. He recognised Andy immediately.

"Well, Andy, dear boy, how nice to see you again." He threw the door open wide. "Come in, come in."

Andy stepped into the large hall and followed his host into a tastefully decorated room where the soft music of a cello concerto drifted like spider's web on the warm sweet-scented air. Andy stood listening, enraptured.

"Good, isn't she?"

Andy just nodded. "Now then, dear boy, to what do I owe the pleasure of this visit? I know it's not a social call."

"I'm sorry to bother you at home, Vivien, but I need some information about the theatre and no one knows more about it than you."

Vivien acknowledged the compliment with a slight nod of the head and a smile. "Flattery will get you anywhere, dear boy. What exactly is it you want to know?"

"It's this – is it possible to make someone up so they would be completely unrecognisable to anyone who knew them?"

Vivien frowned slightly and waved Andy to a chair. "Without a doubt, dear boy, because recognition depends on whom you are expecting to see. For example, an actor on stage is nearly always recognisable because the audience are expecting to see him or her there. If it was someone who was not known in that way and you put him in a situation that would normally be alien to him, then yes, he could be made up so that his mother wouldn't recognise him. Mind you, it would take a very good makeup artist."

"Are there people around that good?"

"Oh yes! Goodness gracious, I can think of several." He thought for a moment and then added. "The best I can think of is a woman, Lucy Slater."

Andy's eyes opened wide. "Lucy Slater?"

"Yes, she really is excellent. Theatre, television, films, she's done the lot. Her brother lives in The Village somewhere."

Andy left with an open invitation to come to dinner at any time. "Just call me, dear boy, and I can assure you it will be the meal of a lifetime."

Andy thanked him and promised he would be in touch.

As he drove slowly back home he thought about what he had just been told. He hadn't expected to hear the name Slater mentioned and it was beginning to look more and more as if Charlie Slater, his sister, and his army pal, Jack Templeton, were all in this together. He would have to check to see whether or not Lucy was in Temsley, but if she was then he was certain he knew who at least three of the Mozart Men were. The point was, what should he do with the information?

CHAPTER 23

A week after his first visit to the hospital Jack received a letter advising him that the results of his tests were available and that an appointment had been made for him for the twelfth. Looking up from the breakfast table he glanced at the calendar on the wall. Lucy put a cup of tea in front of him and saw him look at the date.

"Anything interesting?" she asked.

He handed her the letter. "Back to the hospital next Tuesday," came the uneasy reply. "Must be something serious if they're that quick off the mark."

"Don't start thinking the worst, Jack, it could be nothing."

The truth was that Jack was glad in a way that the hospital appointment was so quick. The sickness was still with him and the headaches were getting worse. He had had only one day off and he was finding it more and more difficult to concentrate at work and was taking pain killers regularly.

"Why don't you have a few days off, love? You look all in."

He looked up. "You know me, sweetheart, I can't let this beat me. Anyway, I don't like taking days off sick."

Lucy sat down at the table looking serious. "Take a holiday, then. They must owe you some time off. We could go away for a few days, somewhere quiet, leave everything behind."

Jack was tempted. The break might do him a lot of good. He smiled and wondered why they hadn't started their relationship years ago. They might have been proud parents by now. He would have liked to have been a dad. 'Oh well,' he thought, 'no point in dwelling on what might have been.' He rapidly made up his mind. "Tell you what, pack a case, enough for two or three days. I'll phone in and have a word with Trevor. There shouldn't be a problem."

She stood up and made for the door. "Right," she smiled, "I'm on my way. Phone him now, before you change your mind!"

An hour and a half later they were driving west to a little village in the heart of Oxfordshire and a country pub known as the Dying Rose. They hadn't booked, but neither thought it would be a problem and it wasn't. They were welcomed with open arms and spent the next few days walking by the river Thames, wandering the streets of Witney or just relaxing in each other's company. By the time they arrived back at Temsley both were feeling pleasantly refreshed, and although Jack's problems were still with him, they hadn't got any worse. The five days spent away had been wonderful. The change of scenery and air had been a real tonic.

Tuesday arrived and both Jack and Lucy were nervous. Both had the distinct feeling that something was horribly wrong even though they never voiced their opinions to each other. As they walked hand in hand across the chilly windy car park, Jack reflected that it was less than two weeks since he had presented himself to the doctors for the first time. They walked through the maze of corridors once more, and having announced his arrival at the desk, they sat on the same long bench. After half an hour a nurse came over and told him that it was his turn and that the consultant would like to see Mrs Templeton as well. They looked at one another, both thinking it could only be bad news. They were right.

The tests had confirmed the presence of cancer. A course of chemotherapy had been prescribed to start the following day. The consultant pulled no punches and made no promises. The cancer had progressed, and although the prescribed treatment might be the answer, there was no guarantee. Surgery might be an alternative if the treatment was unsuccessful, he told them, but there was even less of a guarantee with that option. He went on to explain the side effects such as hair loss and sickness. Lucy heard what the consultant was saying but she couldn't believe he was talking about her Jack. His voice was distant, as though she were in another room and was eavesdropping on someone else's conversation, one that had absolutely nothing to do with her. It was like listening to a radio play or watching a film. He couldn't be talking about Jack. She was going to wake up soon and discover this was all a horrible dream. It was only as they were walking back across the car park that she began to grasp the horrible reality that it was not a dream.

As they climbed into the car Jack realised how glad he was that they had been away together. It had been the first time for them and it could quite easily be the last.

"That consultant thought you were my wife," he remarked as they fastened their seat belts. Lucy, still deep in thought about the news they had just received, nodded. "Will you?" he asked.

She looked up. "Will I what?"

Jack smiled and held her hand. "Be my wife."

Her face lit up. She squeezed his hand and smiled happily. "I thought you'd never ask."

"We'll get a special licence," he told her. "If we leave it too long we may be too late."

She turned in her seat, a look of horror on her face. "Jack Templeton! Don't ever talk like that again," she snapped. Tears glistened in her eyes and she struggled to keep control. "From now on you will have to think positive for both our sakes." She stopped. "And …" She put her hand to her mouth so that he wouldn't see the way her bottom lip quivered.

"And?" he asked, puzzled. "And what?"

She started the engine. "And what?" he repeated.

She switched off the engine and gripped the steering wheel tightly. She hadn't wanted to tell him here like this, stuck in a car park, but now she had no choice. She took a deep breath. "I'm going to have a baby," she whispered.

Jack was stunned into silence for a long moment. "You mean you're pregnant?"

"I believe that is the medical term for it, yes."

A big grin spread over his face. "I'm going to be a father?" He grabbed her hands. "That's wonderful, wonderful news." He laughed and leaned over to kiss her but he was too quick and the seat belt jerked him back upright. He quickly released it. "Is it a boy?" he asked.

Now it was her turn to laugh. "I don't know, Jack, I've only just found out myself."

"That settles it. Two things we have to do – get married and think positive." He clicked the seat belt back on. "Well, come on," he urged, "we have a licence to get."

When they told Charlie of their coming marriage he was delighted and remarked, "The only thing I can't understand is why you didn't get married years ago."

"There is more news, Charlie." Lucy told him. He immediately thought it must be bad news, but before he could say anything she added, "I'm going to have a baby."

"That's absolutely wonderful news," he enthused as he kissed and hugged his sister and then shook the hand of his friend. "I remember how I felt when Sue told me she was expecting Karen."

Lucy and Jack looked at him. Neither had heard him talk of Sue and Karen since the funeral. He saw them looking. "It's all right now, Lucy, really. Over the last few months I have gradually come to terms with," he paused, "their deaths. I can remember them both now without that overpowering sadness." He smiled and raised his eyebrows. "It's ironic, but I think those addicts that smashed the house up actually did me a favour. They stopped me from living in the past all the time. Anyway, enough of that. What about the test results at the hospital?"

Jack quickly assured him that everything was fine and told him that he had to have some treatment which meant having a few days off work but that it was nothing to worry about. Charlie didn't believe a word but he wasn't going to pursue it. He would ask Lucy later. She would tell him what was really wrong.

Four days later they were married in the registry office. Eight people were invited and all attended. The treatment Jack was receiving was producing the side effects the consultant had predicted, but although Jack was feeling worse than ever, nothing would have kept him away from that ceremony. Straight after they were married, they went along to the hospital for his next treatment session. Even though outcomes were looking gloomy, they were both very happy people.

CHAPTER 24

On an unusually warm February day, a Land Rover bumped to a halt in the grounds of the Edgetown brick pits, ten yards from the water's edge. The four men inside peered out of the windows at the sun-dappled water that gleamed like a million diamonds as a gentle breeze ruffled the surface. It looked very pleasant, but they all knew it was colder than it looked.

"If it's as deep as they say, it will be perfect," said the driver. They all clambered out and made their way towards the rippled surface of the man-made lake. The driver spoke again. "Come on, let's get ready. The quicker we find out if it's Ok, the quicker we can put our plans into action."

The others mumbled agreement and went back to the vehicles to don wetsuits and diving gear. The four men were related. Three were brothers and the fourth was a cousin. Apart from family, they all had one thing in common, a passion for diving. For some time they had shared a dream of opening their own diving school and diving club, but a suitable venue, at least one they could afford, had always been the stumbling block. It seemed that this place could be the answer. They had to make their minds up pretty quick or lose the chance of taking it on, which was why they there on that February day.

They chatted and joked as they got themselves ready and then became serious as they checked each other's equipment. It was decided that two of them would make the initial dive, changing over after a maximum of fifteen minutes. Dave and Tom, the two eldest and most experienced, lowered themselves into the water and the exploration began. It was as they had hoped, very deep, and after a few minutes a glance at the depth gauge told them they were at sixty feet and not yet at the bottom. When they finally reached it, the gauge registered eighty-two feet. Although it was darker at this depth, visibility was still reasonably good. Dave tapped his brother's arm and pointed upwards. Slowly they made their way back to the surface, both convinced that this would be the ideal venue to realise their dreams.

As they rose unhurriedly to the surface, Tom saw something strange at about thirty feet. He pointed and started to swim towards what he had noticed, Dave following behind. As they drew nearer they could see that it was a car perched precariously on a narrow ledge. They swam upward making sure they were above it before approaching too close. It was an old BMW and they could see something white through the windscreen. Tom switched on his powerful torch and there, caught in its beam, was a partially decomposed head. Empty eye sockets stared sightlessly at them and a grotesque grin was etched onto the decaying face. They had found Nick Baker.

Within an hour the police had sealed off the area and were waiting for the crane to lift the car from its watery grave. Police divers had confirmed that there was indeed a body in the car and that it had been tied to the steering wheel. A check on the car's registration told them it belonged to Nicholas James Baker of 28F Jackson Close, Temsley.

Colin Burgess received the information as he sat at his desk. Calling Jenny Tate, they made their way to the Jackson Close address. There was no answer to their knocking and peering through the letter box revealed nothing. Colin lifted his foot and with one blow kicked the door in. Carefully they made their way down the passage and into the front room. The whole place was stuffy and smelt of decay. Everywhere was covered in a thick layer of dust. The carpet had been lifted and floorboards taken up, and on the wall an electrical socket hung open revealing a small safe. In the kitchen there was an empty baked bean tin with a push-on lid next to it, plus an empty cornflakes box.

"We need SOCO down here," he told Jenny. "Get on to it will you. It's almost certain that it's Baker in the car. No one has been in this flat for months."

"Could be that Baker has done a runner and wants us to think it's him in the car." she remarked.

"If that's the case, he would hardly have chosen the brick pit to dump the body. It was only pure chance that it was found in the first place. It looks like someone has cleared him out of drugs and cash then shut him up for good."

"Mozart Men?" ventured Jenny.

"They usually give us an account of what they've done, not keep quiet about it."

"Yes, but this is murder."

"So was a crossbow bolt in Mick Snark's throat."

Jenny was shocked. She had completely forgotten about that pervert.

"This was done for a particular reason," continued the Inspector, and if it was the Mozart Men then I can only think of one – Baker recognised them, or at least one of them."

"But that could mean we might have missed something on the videos they sent us."

"It means nothing," Colin snapped, "except that if it was the vigilantes, they have committed two murders. Rough justice is one thing but judge and executioner is something else. We have to find them, Jenny," and for the first time since the vigilantes began their pursuit of rough justice, he really meant it.

Andy Mills heard about the find in the brick pits and was standing at the edge of the sealed-off area trying to get further in. He had a camera slung round his neck, but for the moment there was nothing he could see that would make an interesting photograph. The local television reporters were also there, obviously having the same trouble. As he waited impatiently, a car swept into the grounds and stopped a few yards from him. Colin Burgess and Jenny Tate climbed out.

"Inspector Burgess!"

Colin looked up and inwardly groaned. "Andy! I'm surprised to see you here so soon." The newspaper man raised his eyebrows and ignored the obvious sarcasm.

"What's been found?" he asked. "The whisper is that it's Nick Baker."

"You shouldn't listen to whispers, Andy," Colin replied and went to move away.

"Come on, Colin, give me something. Facts are better than speculation."

The Inspector stopped. "All right, Andy. A car has been found in the pit and it has a body inside it."

"Is it Baker?"

"We don't know yet."

"Was it the work of the Mozart Men?"

Colin sighed, suddenly annoyed at the use of the term. "Again we don't know, but if it was, then I'm sure you would have been the first to know."

Andy cringed at the remark. "Who found the body?"

Colin glared at the reporter. "That's it, no more questions, you'll be informed when we know something definite." He turned and walked away, waving a hand in a gesture that signified the end of the conversation, knowing full well that Andy would speculate as to who committed the crime and then print his speculations.

As he and Jenny reached the water's edge, the crane they had asked for turned into the grounds. It was mounted on a lorry and more than capable of lifting the car out of the water. Twenty minutes later the crane was ready and the divers, complete with communication equipment, disappeared into the water to attach the lifting gear to the car.

Moving to a different position, Andy managed to get some good shots of the crane lifting the car from its resting place. The television crew had also manoeuvred themselves into a better position and were busy filming the event. The car broke free from the surface and swung towards the bank, water cascading everywhere, but it was impossible for Andy to see whether there was a body inside or not. He wondered whether it was the work of the Mozart Men but concluded it was not, as they had always said what they had done and usually filmed it too. Besides, Colin was right, he would probably have been the first to know. Still, the headlines could ask the question. In any case, it would make a good story.

As the car was lowered to the ground it disappeared from view behind the hastily erected screens that were always present in cases like this. Police photographers took pictures from every conceivable angle before the door was opened and they began again when the body, or what was left of it, came into view. The remains were quickly taken away in a body bag.

The boot was opened up and an officer called out. "Excuse me, sir, you'll want to see this." Colin walked over and gazed in. There were two large, sealed, transparent polythene bags. One was full of pills and bags of powder and the other contained a notebook and money, lots of money. "Why on earth would anyone leave that lot there, sir?"

Colin shrugged. "God knows," he replied, but in his mind his thoughts were turning to the vigilantes. This was just the sort of thing they would do, but he couldn't fathom out why, if it was them, they had tried to cover it up. It just didn't make any sense.

Ronnie Thompson finished his shift then drove from the police station to Jack's house on the Edgetown Estate. He wanted to find out how Jack was, but he also wanted to tell him that Nick Baker had been found.

Jack was stretched out on the settee feeling really down when Ronnie showed up. The treatment had made his hair fall out and he had taken to wearing a woolly hat, not just to cover the baldness but also because his head felt cold. He was also feeling very sick. After the niceties of asking how he was, Ronnie told him about Nick Baker being found.

Jack was taken aback. "How the bloody hell did they find him in eighty feet of water?" His speech was slow and his voice was cracked. Talking was an effort and it showed in his face.

"Some blokes went diving there – you know, proper gear, air tanks and all that, hoping to open a club or school or something. Anyway, he's been found. So what do we do now?"

"Do? We don't do anything." Jack closed his eyes for a moment and when he opened them again he added, "He was the one person we didn't tell anyone about. They won't connect it to us, and even if they do, so what? They're no nearer to finding us now than they were at the beginning."

"Should we declare what we did? They might charge someone else."

Jack took some deep breaths and fought to control the sickness that welled up. Finally he replied, "With a bit of luck they might charge a known criminal and get him put away. At least it'll take another scumbag off the streets." He took a few more deep breaths before adding. "But the chances are they'll put it down to us anyway." He closed his eyes again. He wanted to sleep. Ronnie got up and moved to the door.

"I'm really sorry you're not feeling so good, Jack." Turning to Lucy he said, "Look after him, Lucy, he's being missed already."

She smiled. "You can count on it, Ronnie."

Emma Jennings watched the news and was shocked when she saw the car being lifted out of the brick pit and the newscaster saying that the body inside was thought to be that of Nicholas Baker, a local drug pusher. The police were appealing for anyone who had seen Baker in the last six months to come forward. They stressed that any information would be treated with the utmost confidentiality. Emma wondered whether she should tell them about the last time she had seen him, when the police had taken him and his car away. At the time, she thought he had been arrested. No one at the school had seen him since that day and it was assumed that he had been caught and put in prison. The fact that no one had read about it or seen anything on the local news hadn't registered either.

She decided she would phone the number given, but would not go and be interviewed. The thought of her parents finding out that she had tried drugs, even if it was only the once, appalled her. There was also the matter of having had sex with him, even if it was without her consent. She was actually glad he was dead. If it was him, she reasoned, the one way to make sure was to help the police by telling them what she saw that day.

Going into a public phone box in a quiet part of town, she

dialled the freephone number given. A woman answered, and for that she was thankful.

"It's about Nick Baker," stammered Emma, "I saw him on September the thirtieth."

"Are you prepared to tell me your name?" asked the voice.

"No." Her voice wavered. "I'll tell you what I saw, but I don't want my parents finding out."

"All right," soothed the voice, "it's not a problem. My name is Maggie, what shall I call you?"

"Emma," said Emma.

"Well, Emma, the thirtieth of September was quite a while ago, how can you be so sure that it's right?"

"I *am* sure," she said angrily. "The bastard had sex with me after he gave me a pill." Just saying it made her feel as though she was going to cry. Her voice faltered but she managed to keep control. "He was a pusher and a bloody pervert."

"The date could be very important, Emma. Are you absolutely certain?"

"Yes," she shouted, "I said so, didn't I? Anyway, you can always check your records."

"What do you mean, Emma, check our records?"

"It was the day you arrested him. I was outside the flats when the police came. I stayed and watched them put him in the van. One of the policemen drove his car away too."

"What time would this be?"

Emma was beginning to feel nervous, scared that they would be tracing the call as she spoke. "Half past five," she said. "I went there straight from school." Before she could hear the voice again she put the phone down. If they had traced the call they could be on their way to pick her up. She had to get away from this spot. She wanted to cry and desperately needed to talk to her mum, but she was scared and ashamed. She left the phone box and walked home.

When Colin Burgess heard about the call it confirmed his suspicions about Baker's death being the work of the vigilantes. There was no doubt about it, if this girl was to be believed. The police had not arrested Baker on that day or any other day and they had certainly not taken his car. But why did they kill him? Maybe Baker had recognised one of them, as he had first thought. Maybe it had been an accident. He might have fallen in a struggle and hit his head. It was no use guessing. He might know a bit more when the results of the post mortem came through but he wasn't holding his breath, the body was very badly decomposed.

Jenny Tate put her head round the door. "We might have found out who Emma is, sir," she informed him, waving a sheet of paper in the air. He looked up and the speculations he had been indulging in collapsed like a house of cards in a draught. "The notebook that was found in the boot of the car had a list of names in it. Some weren't readable, but the last entry was Emma Jennings and the word 'school' was next to her name."

"She could have given a false name."

"The operator who took the call thinks not. It was too natural and too quick, she said."

"Well, check the schools, Jenny, and see if they have an Emma Jennings on their books. If you come up with a name I want you to go round and see her." He paused. "… but at the school, Jenny. No parents, at least for the time being. We did say any information would be treated with the utmost confidentiality." He picked up a pencil and started to tap the table with it. "You'd better advise her to have a check-up as well. If he had sex with her … well …" He let the words hang in the air. They both knew what the results of such a test could be.

"How many other names could be read on that list?"

"Not too sure about that, sir. Even though it was sealed in a polythene bag there was some water damage."

"Check it out. If you come up with any other girls' names you'd better talk to them as well."

"What about the boys?"

Colin looked up frowning. "Was Baker gay?"

"Not that I know of," she replied, "but the boys might have introduced girls to the pleasures of so-called soft drugs via Baker. They might also have enjoyed their sexual favours."

Colin acknowledged the observation with a nod. "Right, we'll talk to them as well. When you have a complete list, let me know. You will no doubt need help with the interviewing, depending how many names there are, but go easy and keep away from Andy Mills."

She paused at the door. "Why do you think they chose him to be their intermediary?"

He shook his head. "I've often asked myself that question. If we knew the answer we might have solved this case by now."

Jenny left the office wondering how you tell a fifteen-year-old girl to have a check-up because she might have contracted a sexually transmitted disease for which there was no cure. 'Sometimes this job is just too bloody awful,' she thought, 'and all because of scumbags like Baker.'

CHAPTER 25

Jack was still feeling awful. The treatment had been completed and he had expected to start feeling better. The sickness had mostly left him, but the headaches, although not quite so bad, were still a long way from being cured. Lucy had phoned her brother and asked him to visit, the excuse being that Jack needed cheering up, the truth being that she needed someone to lean on, someone she could trust with her worst fears. The welfare officer from the police force had been to see him, as was the custom, and had asked Jack whether he had considered taking early retirement on medical grounds. Jack had been surprised at the question and was now certainly giving it a lot of thought.

The doorbell chimed its two-tone alarm which always made Lucy think of the 'Avon Lady' and she hurried to answer it. Charlie stood there with a smile on his face clutching a bottle of the finest malt whisky. Lucy threw her arms about him, something that was normally reserved for long-term absences, alerting him to the fact that she wanted to talk something out of her system. They greeted one another and she led the way into the lounge where Jack was.

He was lying on the settee, just as he had been when Ronnie visited him, and Charlie was shocked to see the state he was in. He had always talked frankly and honestly to his friend but now he held back. "You look a lot better than I thought you would," he lied.

Jack nodded and smiled weakly. "What you got there?" he croaked.

Charlie looked down at the bottle in his hand as if it was the first time he had seen it. "It's a bottle of the finest, what else?" He saw Lucy shaking her head so he added, "But as you're not feeling too good at the moment, we'll have to save it for later." He turned to his sister. "How's the mum-to-be?"

She smiled. "Getting bigger and uglier every day. June the twelfth can't come quick enough for me."

"Nor me," croaked Jack.

"It's only another four months, sis," Charlie told her.

"That is one hundred and twenty-two days," she retorted. "But I'm not complaining. A child is something we both wanted and before you ask the question again, it's a boy. I found out yesterday."

Charlie hugged his sister. He was a happy man, not only for himself but also for his sister. The only fly in the ointment was Jack's illness. "You'd better get well soon, Jack. We have a lot of celebrating to do."

"Don't you worry yourself on that score," replied Jack, his voice almost a whisper, "but you're going to need more than one bottle."

The chit chat lasted until Charlie had drunk a cup of tea. "Look, I'd better be going, you look whacked out," he announced. Turning to Lucy he said quietly, "Looks like you could do with putting your feet up too."

"You needn't worry about me," she chided, "I've never felt better." Jack lifted his hand in farewell and Lucy added, "Come on, I'll walk you to your car."

When they were in the street Charlie said unhappily, "He looks very poorly, Lucy. Is it just the treatment?"

She nodded confirmation. "They say he should start to feel better with every day from now on. It'll be some time before they know whether the treatment has been effective, but they are very optimistic. He's always been a fit man and a fighter. I'm sure he'll be all right." Tears glistened in her eyes and her voice wavered nervously as she spoke. "It's taken all these years for us to get together and now it might all end too soon. I don't know if he'll even be here when the baby is born." She burst into tears. "Charlie, what am I going to do?"

He hugged his sister again. "Come on, sis, think positive, be optimistic like the hospital." Pulling a handkerchief from his pocket he wiped her eyes. She took it from him and finished the job herself. "Don't let him see you crying, Lucy, he would hate to think he was making you unhappy."

It took a lot of effort to regain her self-control but she managed it. She watched her big brother drive away, not moving until the car turned the corner. She remembered that the last time she had cried was at Sue and Karen's funeral.

Jack did indeed get better and better as the days went by. He discussed it with Lucy and decided to take early retirement on medical grounds, and wondered whether, as he was feeling so much better, it was still an option. Money was not going to be a problem. In his single days he had put together a nice little nest egg, and Lucy was not exactly poor either. They would manage comfortably on the time he had left, however long it was. If they did retire him on medical grounds, he wondered if it meant they considered he was not going to be cured. Oh well, best not to think of that – he would have to think positive like they had agreed in the hospital car park. He desperately wanted to see his son born.

CHAPTER 26

Tracy Devlin still hadn't spoken about her ordeal, apart from the few words when she was first found. Counsellors, as well as her parents, had tried desperately to get her to open up but to no avail. To start with, she wouldn't talk at all, but gradually the words started to emerge until eventually she was able to hold conversations. To some people they might have seemed normal, but to her parents they were definitely not. Something was missing, the spark and the giggle in her voice along with the sparkle in her eye. She hardly ever watched the television or read newspapers, preferring to listen to music or read the books of her choice. She was back at school, but it was clear to those who knew her well that she was different, changed. Her friends supported her but they all recognised that the light in her personality had dimmed considerably.

Chancing one day to walk into the lounge where her parents were watching the news on television, reality suddenly altered dramatically for her. There, on the screen, was Roy Marks, walking to the court accompanied by two police officers, and she saw on his left arm a small tattoo in the shape of a shield. It was an image she could never forget. She had seen it as his arm held her down while the other wielded the cane. She saw it as he thrust into her time and again, and she saw it when he dragged her from the car and dumped her in the road. She stared at the screen mesmerised, for when she looked at his face, pictures of the mask that the 'Teacher' had worn began to flash on and off and she knew that this was her abuser. Her parents were surprised at her interest but said nothing, hoping that this was another one of those breakthroughs that they were told would happen, another small fence that had been successfully cleared. From that moment on, Tracy watched the news and read the papers for any sign of this man. She had to know for certain, but to do that she would have to see that tattoo close up and read the motto.

Unfortunately for Tracy, no further news bulletins, or pictures of the man, showed his arm, at least not uncovered. Then came the bombshell. A news bulletin said that Marks could shortly be a free man because the evidence against him was proving inadmissible. His solicitor was preparing to ask the magistrates at the committal proceedings the following day, to rule that there was no case to answer. Tracy could not believe it. she knew he was the one. She considered telling the police what they wanted to know about her ordeal, but thought that after all this time they wouldn't believe her, and she could not face telling her parents what had happened. She just did not have the words to tell them how that man, dressed as the 'Teacher', had violated her, and she was angry because he could be free the next day whereas she would never be free.

Roy Marks walked from the court a free man. The defence his solicitor presented, that there was no case to answer, was upheld by the magistrates. The fact that Jeff Spooner, Curly Wilson, and the others had said nothing that would implicate him was also a factor in their reaching that decision. As he walked from the court he was mobbed by press and television reporters who shouted so many questions at him he was unable to answer anything. Eventually he managed to say, "Yes, it is my intention to resume work. I have done nothing wrong and the court has cleared me." To another reporter he declared, "No, I don't bear any malice to those who arrested me. They were doing their job and mistakes do sometimes occur." All the while he spoke, he was struggling through the crowd to a waiting car.

Tracy Devlin was in the crowd. She was desperately squeezing herself through the mass of pushing bodies to get near the front, and all the while Marks was getting closer and closer to his waiting car. Still she continued to force a path through the throng. She *had* to see that tattoo. As he reached the car she tugged on the coat of one of the reporters. He was from the local paper and as he looked down at her he recognised her as the schoolgirl who had gone missing for four days during the summer.

"Ask him to show you the tattoo on his left arm," she pleaded tearfully. "It's got a Latin inscription." The reporter was unsure about her request, but he sensed a story so he called out.

"What about the tattoo on your left arm, Mr Marks, the one with the Latin inscription?"

Marks froze and turned to face his questioner. "What about it?"

"Will you show it to us?"

He went white. Anger welled up in him like a tidal wave, huge and threatening, but anger was an emotion he had to keep under control. He wondered what harm it would do for them to see the tattoo? But then he began to wonder how they could possibly know about it. This might be a trap.

"No," he snapped, "I will not."

He struggled forward once more towards the waiting car. Another reporter in the crowd asked the same question, then another, but he said nothing more. All he wanted was to reach the car where he would be safe from questions. He reached it just as Tracy managed to get to the front of the crowd where he was standing. His arm moved towards the door handle and the sleeve of his jacket rode upwards revealing the very thing he had wanted to keep hidden. Tracy saw the movement and the tattoo and knew without doubt that he was 'the Teacher'. She stepped forward into the small space that surrounded him.

"Remember me, Teacher?"

Marks looked down at the girl and he remembered. Oh yes, how he remembered.

"Ignorantia Excusat Peccatum," she called out. A nervous grimace flickered across his face as he realised she knew who he was. As he made a grab at the car door handle, she drew a knife out from beneath her coat. He saw it, but even as he tried to move, he realised it was too late because he was hemmed in by the crowd and the car. A look of fear replaced the nervous smile as the sturdy kitchen knife, its six-inch blade honed to a sharpness that would cut cleanly through a sheet of paper, flashed in the winter sunlight and plunged into his groin. It went through his clothing with ease and sliced into his genitals until it hit a bone.

For a moment, a very brief moment, everything was silent and still. The look of fear that had etched itself onto his face distorted into one of disbelief and then of agony. He screamed and went down on his knees, desperately clutching at the knife protruding from between his legs. Blood started to pour from the wound. Tracy watched without emotion as he writhed on the pavement. Someone in the crowd screamed and then panic ensued. A plain clothes policewoman rushed forward to pick up the girl and pushed her way through the crowd and into the court house. Police ran down the court steps towards the injured man, trying to clear a space. Someone stepped from the crowd declaring he was a doctor and began to administer what first aid he could until an ambulance arrived.

Everything that had taken place had been recorded by the television cameras and they continued to record as the police cleared a path for the ambulance as it sped into the car park where the court house stood, siren blaring and blue lights flashing. Tracy, flanked by three women police officers, watched through the windows of the courtroom. She didn't care, justice had been done and she felt free from the burden of guilt that she had carried since he had abused her. Whatever happened to her now would be nothing compared to what he had done to her. The two men with him were also implicated, but he had been 'the Teacher'. And now the teacher had been taught.

Inspector Burgess and Constable Tate had been at the top of the court house steps as the whole episode took place. When they heard the screams, they rushed down the steps and pushed their way through the crowd, passing the officer who was carrying Tracy into the court. A doctor was there but blood was still pouring out onto the pavement.

"How is he?" Colin asked breathlessly.

"Not good. I think an artery has been cut. Hurry that ambulance up or it will be too late." Colin pushed the transmit button on his radio then stood up to let the doctor get on with whatever he was doing to save Roy Marks' life.

They went back into the court and turning to Jenny he said, "Now what?" She shrugged her shoulders and shook her head. "Suddenly everyone wants to be a vigilante." he grumbled.

"She might have bloody good cause," Jenny snarled.

Colin spun round on her. "Oh, I see!" he exclaimed angrily. "Breaking someone's hands or knees is not Ok but it's all right to stab a man in the street and let him bleed to death." He glared at her as he added, "Or is it just because a girl did it that makes it acceptable."

Jenny turned scarlet. "I didn't mean that at all," she objected.

"Then what exactly did you mean?" he retorted. Waving an arm he said dismissively, "It doesn't matter. Come on, let's see how the girl is."

Roy Marks didn't die but it was touch and go for a while. Tracy was unrepentant. The only thing she was sorry about was that he survived. Jeff Spooner and the others suddenly had a change of heart and all decided to implicate Marks. Their evidence, and a close study of the videos for that tattoo on Marks' arm, was enough to produce another hearing and this time the magistrates found there was a case to answer.

Jack and Lucy had watched the whole thing on the television. They had been incensed when Marks walked out of the court a free man, but were equally deeply shocked when Tracy calmly stabbed him.

"It looks like we've started something," remarked Jack a little sadly.

"I don't think so, love," countered Lucy. "When a girl has been raped and violated all sorts of things happen inside. She would have done that whether or not the vigilantes had existed. In fact I believe I would have done the same thing myself."

Day by day Jack had been getting better and was more or less back to his old self, although he knew the cancer could start up again almost without warning. He had decided to take retirement on health grounds and spend what time he had left with Lucy and, hopefully, their son.

"One thing is certain, love," he whispered. "I won't be doing any more dishing out justice." He looked at Lucy. "Do you think Charlie will want to carry on, or has he had enough too?"

Lucy frowned. "I think Charlie and the others will quit while they're ahead. Anyway, I'm certainly out. My job from now on is you. You are the most important thing in my life, not chasing crooks and other ill-doers."

Charlie also wanted out, but there was one job that he was keen to finish before the vigilantes called it a day – the Oyster Club. They would have already done it if they hadn't been side-tracked by the child killer Snark. They still had the information on the club, but with Jack off sick and now taking retirement there was no way of discovering whether or not it was still valid. After some persuasion from Charlie, and on the strict understanding that not only was she not going on the job, and that it would be the last one, Lucy agreed to do the makeup. Jack voiced no objection, just wished with all his heart she wasn't doing it.

It was a few days before the plans for the Oyster Club were ready. Charlie had decided that a serious lesson had to be learnt by the owners of the club, the Rietti brothers, and wanted the club shut down permanently. Although there was no guarantee from their actions that permanent closure would happen, they could at least guarantee a serious lesson and long-term closure.

The club was an old building that had at one time been used as a social club by the railway, who had eventually sold it on to be turned into a night club. It stood on its own, situated between the rear of the Three Ways pub and the railway warehouses in Mallerton Road. The entrance to the car park and the club itself was in Mallerton Road and between the empty railway warehouses. It was a known haven for drug-pushers, but apart from the small amounts found occasionally on individuals, nothing could ever be proved against the owners, even though the police knew they not only allowed drugs to be sold there but were paid to turn a blind eye. There was also more than a hint of suspicion that they had a hideaway for the drugs in the event of a police raid.

When Lucy got the call that everything was ready, she drove out to the factory unit they used, made up the three men and returned post haste to Jack.

CHAPTER 27

At nine in the morning, towards the end of the rush hour, a familiar white police van turned off the Mallerton Road into the area which housed the railway warehouses. There were seven of these but only the three nearest to the railway lines were used and that was for long-term storage of old unwanted railway equipment. There were no personnel on the site. The used warehouses were checked every evening to make sure there had been no break-ins, but the empty ones were ignored. The van turned right between the unused buildings and stopped at the rear of the club out of sight of the Three Ways pub. Two officers alighted, made for the back door, looked cautiously around and walked in.

A passage led eventually to the main area of the club but the two policemen headed directly for the office, a small room on the right, the windows of which overlooked the back yard. The Rietti brothers were both in the office. They had seen the van pull up but were not unduly concerned as they were too busy counting the previous evening's takings in readiness to take to the bank in the High Street, something they did every morning. They both looked up when the officers walked in.

It was Roberto who spoke. "What the hell are we supposed to have done now?"

A voice with an Irish accent replied, "We would like you to come to the station to answer questions relating to an incident last night involving drugs."

Mario spoke now, frowning. "What incident? We don't

know anything about an incident and we're not going to the station to answer to nothing."

The officer's expression did not change. "In that case, Mario and Roberto Rietti, I am arresting you on suspicion of dealing in drugs and for allowing your premises to be used for the same."

Before either of the two could resist they had been securely handcuffed. Roberto shouted, "What about our fucking money? We can't leave it there."

One of the officers picked up the bunch of keys that was lying on top of the still-open safe. "We will lock up, Mr Rietti. No one will steal your money."

They were hustled out to the waiting van. As the group left the premises, the officer in the van climbed out and opened the rear doors. The brothers were pushed in and made to sit on the floor, the other officers climbing in after them. The van pulled out of the yard and turned left into Mallerton Road. When it reached the junction, it turned right into Temsley Road and then left over the river bridge.

"This ain't the way to no police station," shouted Mario. Neither officer spoke. "Are you fucking deaf, you morons? You're going the wrong way." He tried to stand but with his hands secured behind him that simple task was all but impossible. Silently one of the policemen pushed him roughly back down on the floor. "You're going to regret this, you bastard," shouted Mario, "I can promise you that."

The officer still said nothing, just reached over and blindfolded them both. At that point, Roberto Rietti knew for certain that, whoever these people were, they were not the police.

The blindfold silenced them both for a while and as they sat in the darkness, unable to see where they were going, imagination started to take over their minds and fear began to invade their bodies. When they stopped outside the factory unit they heard the shutters being raised, felt the van moving forward and heard the rattle of the shutters being lowered. Still blindfolded, they were pulled out into the empty interior of the unit. Both men knew something was terribly wrong.

It was Roberto who spoke eventually. "You're not the police."

It was a statement and his brother Mario frowned under the blindfold and turned his unseeing eyes towards his brother's voice.

"Not the police?" he echoed.

"No. They're them vigilantes, the Mozart Men."

Mario drew in a deep breath. "Oh shit!" he whispered. He turned towards where he thought his captors were and called out, "What the hell are you going to do to us?"

The Irish accent was heard again. "That depends on you," it said softly. The words drifted down to them full of menace. "If you lie to us, well ...," he shrugged his shoulders and let the rest of the sentence hang unspoken in the air. "We want to know how many pushers sell drugs in your place, who they are and how much they pay you. Then we want to know why no drugs are ever found when a police raid happens."

Mario shouted, "We don't know what you're talking about. We don't take money from pushers and we don't know nothing about no drugs." His feet were swept from under him and he screamed as he crashed to the floor on his face.

"What about it, Roberto, do we do this the hard way?" Roberto shook his head. "No, there's no need for that," his voice was resigned. He knew he was beaten and that no matter how much the pair of them denied everything, they would eventually tell all. "I'll tell you what you want to know."

A tape recorder was switched on and when prompted with questions, he began to talk. There wasn't much to tell, but he told them the names of seven pushers, gave their addresses and how much they paid each of them to sell drugs unmolested in the club one night a week. He told them there was only one pusher in the club on any one night and if anyone else was caught they were 'dealt with'. He also told them of the hiding place where the drugs were put in the event of a raid – a cupboard set into the wall behind one of the fire extinguishers, but, he added, there was nothing in it now.

Mario moaned as he struggled to get to his feet but he was pushed roughly down on the floor again. Both men were tied hands and feet and the cuffs removed, then they were gagged and pushed back into the van where they lay helpless on the floor. The police signs and the blue lamp were removed and replaced with an orange lamp and a board with the logo *Countrywide Express, Delivery & Storage Specialists*. The police clothing was covered with white overalls, and making sure there was no trace of their ever having been there and that the coast was clear, they drove out of the unit, locked it for the last time and made their way back to the railway warehouses.

While Ronnie busied himself making sure the new name-plates on the van were straight and in order, Charlie and Phil took the keys and went into the club, each carrying a can of petrol. In the office the money was still on the table where it had been left. They collected it up in a carrier bag and after making sure that the building was empty and no one could get in from the front, they checked that the hiding place for the drugs was indeed empty. That done, they poured petrol over everything and made their way to the back door. Returning to the van, they dragged the brothers out and put them in one of the empty warehouses.

Cards were put round their necks declaring what their crimes were. The Irish accent drifted down to them again. "The club is going to be burnt down. You will not reopen it, or any other place like it and if we find out that either of you continues to have anything to do with drugs, you will both be as dead as Nick Baker. This is lesson 1."

A sledgehammer smashed into Mario's right ankle breaking bones, and as he screamed under the gag the same treatment was delivered to Roberto's right ankle with the same devastating effect. Charlie and Ronnie climbed into the van and waited with the engine ticking over as Phil made a trail of the remaining petrol, threw a lighted match on it and hurriedly climbed into the waiting vehicle. As the van pulled away there was a 'whoosh' and the club went up in flames.

They drove the long way round to Slater's garage by turning right into Mallerton Road, right again into the ring road and then right again into the High Street. Having changed their clothes and rid themselves of the disguises and makeup, Phil set about removing the false plates from the van and doing a thorough valeting job on it, Ronnie walked into town and Charlie sat in his office to do some paperwork. It was 11:30 on a Monday morning and most of the town was soon aware that the Oyster Club was a blazing wreck. It was a fireman who found the Rietti brothers, and as Charlie dialled Jack's number, they were being rushed to hospital.

Inspector Burgess was not too concerned about the fire at first, but when he was told that a fireman had found the Rietti brothers with the all-too familiar white card around their necks, he and Jenny Tate were soon on the scene. When they arrived, the fire was under control but the building had been completely gutted and was just a shell. They stood by the empty warehouses gazing at the still-burning building. A high wooden fence separated the Three Ways car park from the railway property and Colin Burgess looked in its direction.

"Bloody hell!" he exploded as he craned his neck. "If you look over the fence you can see the nick from here." He delved into his pocket and pulled out a mint which he popped into his mouth. "They're doing it right under our bloody noses now. Evans will go mad when he hears about this."

He turned and saw Andy Mills walking towards him. "Damn," he muttered, "the local press."

"Good morning, Inspector, is it just a fire or has someone done for the Rietti's?"

Colin thought about telling him to sod off but there was little point as he would no doubt have already received a package containing all the information.

"They've gone to hospital, broken ankles by the look of things."

"Did they say anything? Was it the Mozart Men?"

Colin nodded. "They haven't been questioned yet but it looks as though it's them. The usual white card round the neck was there. Haven't you had anything?"

Andy shook his head. "No, not yet. Still, it's early days." As he turned away he snapped his fingers and said, "When you do question them, find out if someone was humming or whistling Mozart."

Colin was getting distinctly annoyed about the Mozart connection. "Why's that, then? Do you think it's someone in the Mallerton Symphony Orchestra – the conductor perhaps?"

Andy acknowledged the sarcasm. He didn't want to give too much away but he declared, "If they were humming Mozart then I think I know who it is."

Colin raised his eyes, looked at Jenny Tate and called, "Righto, Andy. I'll let you know." Turning to Jenny, he muttered. "That man is getting on my bloody nerves. Now he thinks he's a detective."

What Andy had really wanted to hear was that no one was whistling or humming anything. If that was the case, he would almost certainly know who it was, or rather he would know who one of them was because that person wasn't there. He walked away quite contented, knowing he would solve the riddle of the vigilantes before the police did. He would be able to retire with a great big feather in his cap and might even write a book on how he had tracked down the Mozart Men. The thought of being one up on the police made him smile even though the thought of retirement didn't. Still, it wasn't looking so daunting now.

CHAPTER 28

Three days after the Oyster Club fire Jack took a turn for the worse. He had been doing very well and both he and Lucy thought he was on the mend. He managed to convince himself that the latest set-back was nothing to do with the cancer but was something else that could be cured, even though whatever it turned out to be was making him feel bad at the moment. Lucy was due to take him to the hospital for his appointment that day and so, with a bit of luck, they would know whether the treatment had worked or whether surgery would have to be considered.

Andy Mills went to the police station to see Colin Burgess, or rather he went to the station on the pretext of the weekly report he made on behalf of the newspaper. The report was as usual and included road accidents, burglaries, whoever had been arrested for shoplifting, and so on. He was surprised at just how little there was – two burglaries, one road accident, and only one shoplifter arrested. On reflection, maybe he wasn't really surprised as the crime figures had been going down rapidly since the Mozart Men had started their activities several months back. He asked to see Inspector Burgess and as he was shown into Colin's office a few minutes later, he noticed a hint of smugness on the policeman's face.

"Not much criminal activity this week, Colin," remarked Andy. "It would seem the vigilante tactics are working."

Colin said nothing.

"Did you find out if anyone was humming Mozart?"

The policeman leaned forward over his desk. "No one,

according to the Rietti's, did anything but talk and there wasn't much of that. Did you receive anything from them?"

Andy shook his head. "I was about to ask you the same."

"We never had anything this time either."

"Maybe they've changed their minds, or their tactics."

Colin shook his head. "No. There's no reason for them to alter things. I think that this is a copycat. If it is, then it's thanks to these idiots you dubbed the Mozart Men. It won't help anyone at all if they've started some sort of trend in do-it-yourself punishment." His eyes narrowed and his manner assumed an air of hostility. "If you know something, Andy, or think you know something about these vigilantes, I want you to tell me."

"I don't know anything, Inspector, but I do have an intuition that it's an inside job." He thought to himself, 'In fact I *know* it's an inside job.' He stood up to go.

"If you're withholding information, Andy, I'll throw the book at you."

The reporter, near retirement and not easily fazed, looked back at the Inspector with a slight grin. "I'll bear that in mind," he said.

The following morning Andy made his way to Jack Templeton's address. He knew he was off sick but thought that a chat wouldn't do him any harm. There was no answer to his knocking and no car in the drive either. A neighbour came out of the house next door and before she could speak, Andy called out to her. "Do you know if Jack's all right? I know he's not very well and I can't get any answer."

The woman studied him, trying to decide if she could confide in him. "He's in hospital," she told him. "They took him in first thing. His wife followed in the car."

"Wife!" Andy exclaimed. "I didn't know he was married. He kept that a secret!"

"They've only been married a little while they have. Rather sudden like." She lowered her voice. "I think it's got something to do with his illness." She mouthed the word 'cancer' as though to speak it out loud would somehow cause her to catch it. "He's been very poorly, you know."

Andy nodded understandingly, thanked her and went back to his car.

'Now what?' he thought. 'I can hardly go to the hospital and confront him with what I know. Mind you,' he reasoned, 'if it is cancer, I might not get another chance.' He decided to risk it.

After numerous tests Jack had been settled into a ward with eight other patients suffering with similar problems. Lucy stayed with him of course. Jack felt deep down inside him that he was going to die very soon. He wasn't scared of dying, in one way it would be a release because the pain was becoming worse with every passing hour, but he was saddened because he would never see the birth of his child. 'At least,' he thought, 'the wonders of modern science have been able to tell me that my child is a boy.' That knowledge partially contented him.

Lucy told him she would go and have something to eat in the hospital canteen and stood up to leave him for a while. Jack reached out and touched her tummy. She was very big now and he could sometimes feel the baby kicking, which was a joy to him. He closed his eyes, not to sleep but to relax. The pains he was getting were sometimes quite bad and he had refused morphine because he wanted to be aware of his surroundings and of Lucy for as long as possible. Pain killers, he thought, would rob him of that awareness. As Lucy left the ward she passed the bulk of Andy Mills, a man whom she thought she recognised but couldn't place. As she struggled with her memory a nurse asked if she was all right, breaking into her train of thought. She smiled and assured her that everything was fine and carried on towards a much-needed cup of tea and a sandwich, all thought of the ponderous man dissolved by that simple enquiry.

Andy headed for the ward that Jack was in, having made enquiries at the desk. He passed the pregnant woman in the corridor, noticing that she was giving him a questioning look, but he didn't think anything of it. Turning into the ward he saw the two rows of beds and began to look for Jack. He couldn't see him at first and then he suddenly recognised him, lying on the bed with his eyes closed. He was shocked at what he saw and could hardly believe that this was the traffic warden who had been humming Mozart just a few months ago. His face had sunk in and his skin was grey. His arms, which were lying on top of the covers were like matchsticks and his head had a dark shadow on it where the hair was trying to re-establish itself once more and failing miserably. A woman's coat was draped over the back of a chair.

He stood at the foot of the bed, struggling with himself about whether he should continue with his enquiry. The urge to know the truth and bring it to a conclusion was very strong, but the urge to leave this man in peace was also very strong. As he started to turn away he heard a voice, or rather a croaky sound imitating a voice.

"Hello, Andy." He turned back to see Jack looking at him with a hint of a smile tugging at his cracked lips. "What does the local paper want with me?"

The reporter hesitated. The question was also an invitation to talk so he replied, "Oh, I just thought we could have a chat."

"What about?"

"How about the latest crime figures?"

Jack smiled weakly. "I understand they're pretty good, down a lot on last year's."

Andy nodded. "And we both know why, don't we?"

Jacks voice went to a whisper. "The Mozart Men, Andy," he croaked. "That's why."

"I know who they are, Jack. Well, three of them anyway." Jack stayed silent. "There's you, and Charlie Slater and his sister. There has to be at least two more of you but I have no idea who they are." Jack coughed painfully and pointed to a glass of water with a straw in it. Andy picked it up and held it while he drank. When he put his head back on the pillow he spoke.

"What makes you think that, Andy?" He tried to sound affronted but only managed to sound tired.

"Easy, Jack. You supplied the information and possibly some equipment. Charlie supplied the van and the factory unit south of the river, and Charlie's sister is the makeup expert, one of the best in the business."

"You're wrong there, Mr Mills," came a cool female voice. "I am the *best* in the business." Andy spun round to find the pregnant woman he had passed in the corridor standing at the foot of the bed. "I am also Mrs Templeton," she added.

"Just suppose you're right, Andy," croaked Jack, "what are you going to do about it?"

The question surprised Andy, mainly because he realised he didn't know the answer. What he had found out might be able to be proven, or it might not, but the one thing that was certain was that Jack Templeton would never stand trial even if it could be proved he was the man behind the whole thing.

"Do?" he whispered. "I don't know what I would do." He mulled it over in his mind. If he blew the whistle and the vigilantes were put out of action, what would happen? The crime figures would certainly go up again, maybe even more so. What had they done anyway – beaten some young tearaways and thieves? Yes, but they had deserved that. Broke Bannerman's hands? Yes, but he deserved that too. What about Hartley? Yes, he had to be stopped and the law couldn't do that. In his mind he listed the other things they had done and then he came to Baker and Snark. He looked at Jack, so thin and weak.

"There were two murders, Jack – Baker and Snark."

Lucy interrupted. "Snark was a murderer, Mr Mills," she snapped, "and so was Baker. We know of at least two youngsters who died because of the drugs Baker was supplying. He was also HIV positive and indulging in under-age sex with schoolgirls. I wonder how many young girls will die because of his perversion." She walked round the bed and sat on the chair opposite.

Jack spoke feebly. "You're not going to say you're against capital punishment are you, Andy, not after the articles you wrote on the subject in that newspaper of yours." He coughed and his body shook with the effort.

"Is that why you sent me the stuff you did, because of my articles on crime and punishment?"

Jack ignored the question. "Baker and Snark were rubbish," he croaked, "and we both know they would have killed again."

"So, are you admitting to being the Mozart Man?" Andy asked.

Jack looked at Lucy. "How would you like to get me a bar of chocolate, sweetheart?" She looked at him questioningly, a scared look on her face. "It's all right," he whispered. "Really."

"I'll be five minutes," she said fiercely, looking straight at Andy Mills, then turned and walked out of the ward.

Jack took some deep breaths. The pain was quite fierce now and he had to get himself under control. "Have you got a tape recorder hidden on you, Andy?" The reporter looked shocked but he stood up, took his coat off and draped it over the woman's coat on the chair beside the bed.

"No, there's no tape recorder."

Jack coughed again. "You're right, Andy, at least about me. I am the Mozart Man you wrote about. I'm not going to tell you who else was involved and I can assure you, you won't be able to prove a thing." He coughed harshly once more. "The vigilantes will die with me, Andy, and if the news gets out, you will be responsible for a renewed increase in the crime rate. As far as Snark is concerned, you will never be able to tie that in with me. I have witnesses, senior police officers, who will swear that I was in my office at the nick on that day and at the time he was killed." More coughing wracked his frame. "Baker was different though," he finally managed to say. "We never said officially that it was us so you will have to guess about that." He closed his eyes tightly, the pain was almost violent now.

"What triggered it off, Jack? Why did you suddenly start taking the law into your own hands?"

Jack shook his head and coughed again.

"That's enough, Mr Mills." Lucy was back. "He's told you all he's going to and now you must leave us in peace."

Andy opened his mouth to object, but Lucy stopped him. "Goodbye, Mr Mills."

He got up and put his coat on, then bent down towards the prone figure. "I don't believe a word you've told me, Jack. If you're the Mozart Man then I'm the prime minister."

Jack lifted his hand and a weak smile made its way to his ravaged features.

Andy Mills did nothing with the information he had. He couldn't actually prove anything and he was certain that there would be all sorts of contingency plans for the group if they thought they were near to being discovered. He didn't anyway want to see Jack's pregnant wife faced with a prison sentence, or Charlie Slater come to that. What would be the point?

Two days after Andy's hospital visit, Jack died. He passed away with his hand on Lucy's tummy waiting for his son to kick. A week later his funeral took place at the local crematorium. Andy crept in at the back and stood in one corner as the service took place. There were no seats left and hardly any standing room. The chapel was full to overflowing. Jack Templeton had been a well-liked man. Lucy was his only relative, and his unborn son of course. The Chief Constable had turned up to say what a hardworking and upright man he had been.

"There will be no hymns," he told the congregation, "but there will be music played. One of Jack's favourite pieces." As he walked back to his seat the second movement of Mozart's Piano Concerto No. 21 drifted over the assembled crowd. The curtains parted as the coffin slid quietly forward, then closed slowly and silently together again. The Mozart Man had said his final farewell.

"Goodbye, Jack," whispered Andy Mills as he walked out into the spring sunshine. "Goodbye."